THE DROWNING MACHINE

and other obsessions

EMMA E. MURRAY

UNDERTAKER BOOKS

www.undertakerbooks.com

The story, all names, characters, and incidents portrayed in this production are fictitious. No identification with actual persons (living or deceased), places, buildings, and products is intended or should be inferred.

Copyright © 2025 by Emma E. Murray.
All rights reserved.

No part of this publication may be reproduced, distributed, or transmitted in any form or by any means, including photocopying, recording, or other electronic or mechanical methods, without the prior written permission of the publisher, except as permitted by U.S. copyright law. For permission requests, contact Undertaker Books.

Cover art by Matthew Revert.
Interior art by Brett Mitchell Kent.
Formatting by M. Halstead.

First edition 2025.

Reading advisories available in back matter for those who would like them.

For Vera

INTRODUCTION

BY J.A.W. MCCARTHY

Emma E. Murray is not afraid.

She's not afraid of the monsters lurking in the furthest corners of night, the gods who demand unspeakable sacrifices, the machines that kill their creators, the disappointment that comes after getting the one thing you want most. She is not afraid of bodies tearing apart in acts of desperation, of beating hearts and drowning lungs as nourishment. There is an *I see you; we are not so different* vulnerability within the troubled minds of Murray's characters, an embracing of obsession that is uncomfortably familiar as it digs into our own darkest secrets and desires. She knows the most nutrient-rich morsels flourish in the dark.

Of course, as lovers of horror, we're not necessarily afraid to follow Murray into that darkness. We stand behind her, thrilled, repulsed and heartbroken all at once, as she guides us through the lives of people cleft by desperation, pummeled by loss, buoyed by a barbed hope that births the kind of actions that seem unthinkable until we're fully in their skin. It's easy to slip into the skin of a character who nurtures a severed limb as a whole, living child when that character is penned by Emma E. Murray.

We are all afraid of loss, as the stories in this collection illustrate, so perhaps that is Murray's one fear, even as she faces it head-on. Loss is felt most acutely in the presence of love, so that leads me to another fear we share as humans, even as we spend our lives chasing it: love.

Yes, I realize I'm dangerously close to unravelling my own theory. Still, I maintain that Emma E. Murray is fearless as a writer. She certainly knows fear well enough to unsettle her readers, immersing us in all the gruesome details of flesh and muscle and sinew, keeping us turning the pages with adrenaline-fueled fervor. She knows fear well enough to have danced with it, dismantled it, and rebuilt it with all its bile-drenched vulnerabilities proudly displayed on the outside.

The theme of loss remains an anvil over our heads, shadowing every step we take, and Murray's writing shows she experiences it no differently. Because we fear loss, we as humans tend to fear love. We wrap ourselves in the armor of indifference, soothe our tender hearts by distancing ourselves from those closest to us, justifying our cruelties with the good old chestnut of "you're better off without me." This is the space in which Murray forces our eyes open, holds us to the page and ensures that we feel everything. This is where Murray's fearlessness shines brightest.

Emma E. Murray is not afraid of love.

Monsters, serial killers, kidnappers, grotesque omens from the heavens—they hold no dominion over us if we remain afraid of love. You wouldn't fear the noose if you didn't have anyone or anything to live for. You wouldn't find power in pain if you didn't love yourself enough to fight for your autonomy.

Because Murray is not afraid of love, these stories hit hard. The women and children in *The Drowning Machine and Other Obsessions* draw great strength from their love even as they face the very human terror of losses staggering enough to shatter the soul. In these stories, love is the driving force, the flesh and bone machine that inspires a child to sacrifice herself for another, a teen to mutilate herself at the urging of a manipulative god, a woman to do the unthinkable in order to protect her child. They tear themselves open, unafraid of their vulnerability, unashamed in their need. These characters may break, but they put themselves back together, even if it's in ways we're afraid to imagine.

From mothers who sacrifice themselves to the unknown for their children, to women who will do anything to become one with what they desire, this collection is an unflinching cornucopia of terrible acts rooted in a love so bright it burns away the resulting pain. Reason is eclipsed, consequences inconsequential compared to the goal: the thriving survival of what these characters love. A love so all-consuming these characters march eagerly into the flame.

So we follow Murray through these pages, these lives. We see the strength that comes from letting love in, and the horrors of fighting to save it. When love finds you, you fight like hell to keep it. You preserve an image, a body part, an echo of a perfect moment, all at the expense of your health and sanity. You crack your chest open, nestle what you love next to your heart, feed it with your blood, use your fear to render your flesh as the ultimate nourishment, your body as feast and seawall. After reading these stories, you can easily picture yourself gnawing off your own arm, not to save yourself, but to save the love that you once feared.

All this to say, *The Drowning Machine and Other Obsessions* is not only a horror collection; it's a collection of love. And what could be more terrifying? Heartache may be the greatest human horror, but it's also an invitation.

Eyes open. Hurry up. Emma E. Murray is holding the door open for you.

— J.A.W. McCarthy
October 2024

I

AN ANGEL OF GOD

The day after St. John died, swaddled in my arms, was the day the airplane crashed in the valley. I'd just finished washing his tiny form in the basin and was getting his clothing ready while he lay wrapped in one of the good towels, his slack face drying under the cloudless sky. I had the onesie from Mamaw in my hands, smoothing it between my fingers and wondering how the sky could be so beautiful when the heavens should've been opening up to weep, when I saw something come sailing into the valley, just above the treetops and silent as a monk.

I had to shield my eyes. The soundless figure was a blip of white haloed by sunburst. My breath caught in my throat. I was sure it was an angel of God, but then it changed before my eyes. It became a plane, the small kind that rich folk like to show off in. I watched as it drifted down, a white whisper into the treetops, and disappeared into the foliage. The mountains echoed with the roar of limbs ripping from their trunks and a flurry of birds scattered into the air. Then all was quiet again, as if it hadn't happened at all.

For a while, I pretended like it hadn't. I dressed St. John in a clean cloth diaper and then the terrycloth onesie with a yellow duck embroidered on the chest. The last thing from Mamaw before she passed not long after I found out I was with child. I combed the wisps of fawn-brown hair on his two-month-old head and held him close to me, rocking him in my arms as I walked slow and deliberate to the grave I'd dug with my trowel and my own hands.

There was no reason to find a way into town for a funeral. Nobody was left to attend save myself. No reason for a plot in the churchyard with the family. That'd be too far for me to visit as often as I'd want to, so I knew I had to bury him down from the house, near the little creek. It was pretty there, shady and the ground was soft and mossy. Sure, the preacher wouldn't approve, but he's wrong about a lot of things. That's why I don't waste my time there anymore. No, this would be better. A comfortable place for his head to rest, under the earth but forever nearby; a little wooden cross to mark it with his name written as pretty as I could. The name I'd picked from my favorite book from school; a good and honest man's name who was also taken too young.

My hands shook as I set him down, but I couldn't bring myself to cover him. Not yet. His placid face, already darkening from that disrespectful, violent hand of death. No, I couldn't do it. I didn't say a word, but my heart prayed louder than my voice ever could. *Please God, give him back. I can't take it.* And that's when I heard the sound of the Lord calling me.

High-pitched, thin screeching, like when a frog or fish has the life squeezed out of them, but much louder and full of terror; it wasn't at all the glorious sound I'd expected from an angel, and yet I instinctively knew what it was. I couldn't leave St. John there, for fear some wild thing would carry him off, so I wrapped him in a blanket and set him in his cradle in the bedroom before hurrying out to follow the sound.

My heart throbbed against my breastbone as I stumbled through the tall grass and weaved between trees. I felt my pulse behind my eyes, and my temples and 'round the nape of my neck ran with a cold sweat as if I was fevered. No pastor had ever preached about that, but I knew it was the angelic voice that caused it, along with the nausea and racing thoughts, flashing through my mind like secret messages written in light. Entranced, I followed the sound into the valley, where the plane had gone down.

It was easy enough to find once I got close. Though the canopy had enveloped it from above, below a trail of dangling branches and ruin led me along. The wings had been shorn from its sides as soon as it'd entered the forest. They lay in strange angles, tossed into the embrace of the trees. Farther down, I could make out the fuselage, unnaturally white among the dappled shadows. The otherworldly sound had dulled to an irritating hum, like a child's shriek muffled through a pillow.

I climbed through tangles of undergrowth to reach the wreckage and peer inside. My still-healing womb ached with the exertion, but I continued on. Branches had snaked through the windshield and caught the pilot in their arms, winding through his open mouth and pinning him to the seat. A heavy headset threatened to slip off, trails of blood congealing down his face. His eyes were concealed by sunglasses, and I thanked the Lord in a hushed whisper that I did not have to witness their lifeless stare. That was when I realized the sound was not coming from inside the cockpit but farther into the forest. My mind was suddenly bombarded with images of torture and agony, and I knew I was close to finding the angel.

Slinking through the branches, crawling over logs while insects rose in anger and scurried across my hands, twigs catching in my hair and etching faint lines of blood across my face, I continued through the dense brush, thick and undisturbed by the airplane. I knew he was there ahead. I heard the monstrous voice calling me, though it was weak. Then I saw the angel.

His arms were stretched out between two trees, and he hung between them like Jesus on the cross. From his bowed head, beneath the blood-streaked mop of hair, his mouth gaped open and the terrible, inhuman sound still ushered forth, though cracking and weaker than ever. His lower half was missing, nowhere to be seen in the rubble around, and his intestines draped down in red ropes, waterfalling to the forest floor. Behind him, beams of sunlight peeked through the trees and backlit him in holy light.

He didn't look like I'd expected based on all the sermons, Christmas cards, and illustrated bibles I'd seen, but still I knew he was an angel. The moment I saw him, a voice like a thousand voices boomed in my mind and told me, through the voice of the Lord, that this horrid creature was sent just for me.

His eyes were closed, and he didn't seem to notice when I approached, though I wondered if perhaps he was too deep in prayer, communing with God about what would happen next. It occurred to me that angels often appeared as a sort of test, making sure you were worthy of the miracles they came to bestow, so I set to work immediately on freeing him. Careful hands dislodged the tangled intestines from the bushes before lifting him from his perch, climbing back down to carry him home. It was difficult to carry him, though he was not as heavy as I'd expected. I never realized how much weight our legs held. Still, my shirt was soaked with sweat by the time the house came into view.

The angel still hadn't opened his eyes, but I felt his ragged breath against my chest while I carried him, though I was relieved his terrible noise stopped as soon as I had removed him. Laying him across the kitchen table, carefully coiling his innards into a neat bunch and placing them beneath him, I set to work straight away. I wrung warm water out of clean cloths, using the good towels even knowing they'd be ruined. I'm no nurse, but I knew I had to keep everything from drying up. I wrapped his waist in plastic wrap, carefully pressing the wet towels around him first, and waited. He remained silent save some wheezing through the first couple hours and the first time I changed out the wound dressing.

I felt strange in my house with two heavenly, muted bodies. A heaviness grew on my shoulders, and I fiddled with my hands, unsure of how to keep from being idle. I washed the used towels and hung them to dry, hoping it'd happen quickly in the breeze so that I'd have them ready again for the next cleaning. As I was wiping down the sink, wringing the red, tainted water from the rag before wetting it again, I heard a gasp behind me. My whole body shuddered as the wincing, high-pitched screech that had brought me to the angel rang from him again, though quieted to a near whisper by his strained throat.

I wheeled around, grasping the sink behind me as my legs weakened under his haunted stare. He seemed to look through me to another plane, yet still I pushed through my fear and forced him to lock eyes with me. I knew it worked because my mind seemed to fuse with his in a sudden flash of white light and warmth. I cried out in the brief moment of ecstasy, but he looked frightened and confused, and I realized he might still be testing me, so I composed myself.

His lip quivered as he tried to speak, but only fragmented sounds escaped in the same hoarse squeaks as before. His eyes roved my face, searching for comprehension, and I wondered if he was speaking a celestial language I couldn't understand.

"Shh, there, there. I'm taking care of you. Here, drink some water." I offered the cup I'd readied to his lips, but he took only the smallest sip before gagging and turning his head away. "Tell me what you need and I'll fetch it. I want to help you." Then it was my turn to tremble as I leaned closer, feeling his breath hot on my face as I whispered in his ear, "Tell me what I need to do so you'll bring him back."

His mouth continued to move in shapes as if he were speaking, but there was nothing except the noise. I turned my head, nearly pressing my ear against his lips, trying to make any sense of his labored sounds. Then I heard something resembling words, like a whisper through static. I closed my eyes and forced them into real words, teasing out his command until my mind flooded with the image of a stained-glass window I'd seen as a child, depicting an angel with wings outstretched against a blue sky.

"A stained glass? But I don't know how." I looked at him,

pleading with my eyes, but he stared back in the same distant way.

I fell to my knees and threw back my head, my neck long and craning as I prayed for guidance. The orange-red rays of sunset sprayed through the kitchen window and fell across the angel, bathing him in light. I understood. God revels in the creations of man because it is through him it is created.

After fitting the bed with sheets and tucking him in to rest, I quickly gathered every glass and bottle in the house, laid them on the kitchen floor covered by the spare sheet and hammered them into broken pieces. Green olive oil and wine bottles, brown beer bottles, the yellow sunflower that decorated Mamaw's old wind chime, and the cobalt blue glassware that had been an early wedding present before Samuel ran off; I took them all and smashed them into puzzle pieces to be assembled. I knew I couldn't craft a stained glass with no practice or skill, not like the angel I'd seen in the chapel, but I tried a different approach with the materials I had.

The cement mixture slopped in the white bucket as I stirred it in the early evening twilight, the stars just beginning to speckle the sky and a light rain misting down. I poured it into the make-shift mold I'd sawed and pieced together, stomping the pieces of plywood into the mud until they stuck in the shape I'd envisioned. Then I scrambled to arrange the glittering pieces into something beautiful. An angel.

I rushed into the house once more, feeling the burning of the Holy Spirit flowing through my veins, and hurried to find more of my most precious and beautiful objects to add to the artwork. The small white shells from when I visited the ocean as a child, the mother-of-pearl buttons I'd been saving for my favorite sweater, the red glass earrings, and the fake diamond ring that had sparkled in the sun when I showed it off and lied that it was real. I added these all, sliding them into the thickening mixture, arranging them in neat lines and geometric patterns that radiated out through the angel's wings. By the time I finished, the rain had stopped, and the cement had hardened too much to rearrange anything, so I forced myself away to go change the real angel's dressings, telling myself it'd look better when it could sparkle in the morning light. Not just a collage of trash, but something worthy of the Lord.

However, I couldn't sleep a wink, and lay on the floor, one hand in the cradle on my son's chest, listening to the quiet breathing of the angel above us on the bed. When the first rays of sun fell through the cold morning air, I ran outside to see my masterpiece.

It wasn't beautiful at all. A monstrosity, childlike and embarrassing. But wouldn't the Lord see my effort, and knowing my limitations, see the beauty in what I was able to create with my own humble hands?

The morning glowed as the sun rose over the mountains, but there was a stale stagnation, barren and foul, in the air. Perhaps it wasn't enough. I knew the angel would be disappointed before I even entered the room, but when I saw his far-off look, his breath shallow and his brows forced together in a tight frown, I wept. I fell from his side and crawled across the floor to the cradle where St. John lay, his skin more mottled and his face barely recognizable as my little sunshine.

Above us, I heard a sputter and then a low moaning. I pulled myself back to my feet and stood at the foot of the bed. I noticed blood and fluids seeping through the towels and plastic wrap, puddling around him and soaking into the sheets and mattress. His face was blanched, and I thought about all the blood he'd lost from the injury and subsequent wound dressings, but could an angel die? I bit my lip.

I gathered the angel in the blanket and into my arms, cradling his half-body like an infant as I carried him through the house and into the front yard to behold my offering. He instinctively clung to me with the little strength he had left, arm draped over my shoulder, and I noticed he was much cooler than before, almost cold to the touch. As we stepped into the orange morning, my eye caught two planes circling the valley like vultures.

I had to coax him to open his eyes, parting in a squint from the rising sun and scanning briefly across my sparkling master-piece before closing again. There was no change in expression or evidence he'd seen what I'd worked so hard on all night. Something inside me dropped like a weight in my stomach, and anger churned in the burning bile, but wrath is a sin and I knew the Lord was still testing me. Gently, I brought the angel back inside, nestled him into the quilts on the bed, and forced a dribble of water into his mouth with an eyedropper along with some baby Tylenol, even though I knew it wouldn't help much.

"Please, I tried my best. I really did. Now, help me. That's why you came, isn't it?" The words were scarcely a whisper in my dry, tight throat as I watched the angel's eyelids flutter, but he didn't answer. I clutched my hands into fists against my thighs. Swallowing the sob building in my throat, I threw myself across the room to my baby's cradle and tore his tiny, cold form from it, holding him against my chest.

I swung my body back toward the deformed creature on my bed and scowled, my lip rising high and my mouth bitter with venom.

"Are you what I get after all these years of prayer, faith, and absolute devotion? Where's my miracle? Look at my son. You asked for art, and I made it. I passed your test. I did everything I was supposed to my whole life. Now bring him back!" The words gushed out along with streams of tears and mucus. I fell to my knees, gasping for air between heaving sobs. "I'm sorry. I'm so sorry. Just, please, look at him. Please."

On my knees, baby still pressed to my bosom with one arm, the other hand raked across the sheet, clawing toward the angel. "He's more beautiful than anything else I could ever make. I'm no artist, but I'm a mother. That's what you made me, Lord. Give him back. Please, just once. Just this once."

The words disintegrated into guttural sounds and wheezes, but the angel turned his head and opened his eyes. I knew he saw my son: his discolored skin, his distending belly, his still chest. A fly landed on his face and tried to enter his nose, but I waved it away, holding back a curse. He saw that death was eating away at him and soon there wouldn't be enough to come back. Lazarus was empty four days, and my little St. John had already been gone for nearly two. My eyes pleaded with the angel; my every breath begged him.

He craned back his neck and fully opened his eyes, and when I followed his eyeline, there was the small painting hung over my bed of Jesus on the cross. Something inside me clicked, and I knew this was a sign.

I took St. John out to the barn first, swaddled in his bassinet, which I placed in the corner after sweeping away the straw. As I walked back to the house, tires crunched along the gravel road and men's voices drifted up in fragmented echoes from the valley. My blood raced through my veins, spurring me to hurry with my work.

The broken angel was hardly human at all by this point, having morphed in his dying into his true, strange, and unearthly appearance. His skin a translucent pale like a cave salamander, the blue of his circulatory system showing as if through frosted glass. The plastic wrap holding his guts in place had yellowed with fluid and pus, hanging loose and soggy, and the pink of his intestines peeked through, threatening to burst forth. His breathing was so slight as to only be perceived by a hand close to his nose to feel the faintest puff of air, no longer rabbit-like but slowed as if he were holding his breath to conceal the glimmer of life still within. When I picked him up in my arms, I felt beneath the cool flesh something like the flicker of a flame.

As I walked him to the barn, I could see movement in the trees of the valley and more voices. I knew I had to work quickly. I laid him on a bed of straw while I tugged and dislodged the long, thin beams of the wall with a hammer. The roof groaned in protest to its shifting weight. I fashioned the cross on the floor, and then I dragged the angel's temporary body to its final position, his limp arms easy to manipulate and his head lolling back and forth only a moment before resting his chin against his chest. Light flooded my mind with every blink, incorporeal bells rang in incessant, painful reverberations, and a frantic energy crescendoed inside me. I needed to make a sacrifice of my own.

I took the knife and forced it through my left palm, and then struggling to do the same to the right while blood pumped hot and slippery from the wound. All around his body, I dripped and splattered blood before bending down to smear crosses in each cardinal direction. When I stepped back, it was already more achingly beautiful than I would've expected; my pain painting it more vibrant than even the doors of Passover.

I tore the soiled wrappings from his body and watched his intestines unfurl in pale coils around him. Flies had already begun to gather, and I swatted them away from his face and wounds as I carefully arranged the tendrils of flesh into the illusion of draping wings behind him. It was glorious to behold, and I felt the overwhelming warmth of God building inside the barn. I knew it was time for the final touch.

Gathering straw around the foot of the cross, I had only to send one small spark from the lighter and all went orange with flame. The angel didn't move as his form caught fire. Thick, black smoke bellowed out around him, and I watched the angel transform into its true blazing form of God's love before scrambling to drag the bassinet out the barn door.

Behind me, I heard the footfalls of people running and their shouts. I didn't look. Instead, my eyes were on the angel, already darkening into the ash masterpiece I'd designed. They were asking about the smoke, the plane, crying out in despair and confusion, but my eyes had moved to my son. Trembling hands grabbed at my open jaw, tears running down my cheeks.

"He's breathing," I whispered, drowned out by their terrible chorus around me. "Praise the Lord! Look! His chest is moving!"

IF I CARRY YOU

A drizzle collects on the window and runs down the glass while the doctor speaks. I'm holding Katie's hand. Tubes and wires snake around her, burrow beneath skin. Her chest rises and falls with the rhythm of deep sleep.

"We'll set everything up with hospice. They'll make her comfortable. All you have to do is love on her."

"Okay," I say, but I don't feel the words on my lips. My entire body goes numb.

Katie snores a little in her sleep. The sheets crinkle as she stirs. The doctor tries to put his hand on my shoulder, but I slip away. Sweat beads across her brow and upper lip. With an edge of the sheet, I wipe it away. Inside me is nothing. I curl my toes, trying to clench the floor through my shoes, as if I don't, I might float away.

It's nice back at home without the injections and tubes shackling her to the bed. Her freckles come back with afternoons in the backyard. She giggles and plays like a child of nearly four should. Her smile returns, but always thin, always tentative. Like she knows.

Then one morning, a new pain creeps in. The nurse gives her something, but she still rubs at her belly and chest.

"Momma, it hurts."

"I know. I'm sorry." I hold her close to my chest, tears soaking through my shirt. "I'd take it away if I could."

The good days fade and we huddle together under sheets, sleeping when we can. I don't understand how a child so little can handle so much.

I watch Katie sleep. The nurse sets her hand on my arm and takes a breath, holds it a moment. I know what she wants to tell me.

"No, don't."

The words float between us, stark and bare, something unspeakable. She nods, her face pinched, starts the drip and leaves. I curl up on the bed next to Katie and watch her chest rise and fall. I watch her all night, and before the dawn is more than a hint of pinkish gray, I feel her begin to winnow away.

My fingers scrabble for her hand, clench it too tightly, but her eyelids merely flutter as she drifts back into sleep.

"No. Please," I whisper. She answers with a sputtering cough that still does not wake her.

The minutes stretch into hours. Her teeth clatter together, a soft sound like dice in a velvet bag, her lips tinged blue. I pull the quilt around her, rubbing her to keep her warm, begging her to stay.

"I can't do it, Katie. You can't leave me."

My heart splinters, the shards piercing through me. I have to do something. A spark of electric blue bolts across my field of vision, the anguish so intense it's visible.

Her last breath approaches. It circles us. I can feel it with every part of me that had once lived just to grow her, make her whole. And then something in me is changing. Something drastic is necessary, and my body acquiesces.

A shiver crawls through my mesentery, ripples into muscle and the marrow of bones. I feel myself opening. My ribcage expands, tearing skin with the quiet rip of cloth pulled apart, the threads torn from each other in unwoven ragged edges. There is a faraway pain, but my love eclipses it. I can save her.

She whimpers, pleading like a puppy who's not yet opened her eyes. My torso has fully opened, and there's an excruciating cold as my organs beat and writhe, exposed. I take Katie in my arms, setting her against my pounding heart. My ribcage embraces her as I tuck her limp limbs in, curl her up so small as to fit inside me again. There's a shift and stretching as my organs make room around her, sticky sliding as they rearrange around her delicate face. My hips unhinge as my body morphs to create a perch for her. She nuzzles against my liver. Her fingers reach up and graze my spleen. Her eyelashes flicker in butterfly kisses against my ballooning lungs. I look down, hold her, and she releases a tiny sigh, but it's not her last breath. She's relaxing, falling asleep within me, like she did all those years ago.

I close around her. She still threatens to slip away, but I won't let her. My veins and arteries slither into her and bring her oxygen. My stomach melds against her to share our sustenance. As my body fully encases her, I dream of a new placenta growing beside her—an organ specifically to maintain her homeostasis, her life.

I feel her mouth working from within, full of blood, but I know what she's saying. She forms the words, "Thank you, Momma." A sob flows through me and I trace my fingers across my swollen belly, the seam of thick scar tissue already growing to tie me together again.

On trembling legs, I push myself off the edge of the bed and stand. The familiar aches and heaviness of pregnancy overwhelm me, but there's a smile on my lips when I pat my belly, savoring the movement within as she settles against my spine, stroking me back through layers of muscle and flesh.

I cradle her inside myself and on buckling knees, carry the child within myself, never to let her go again until my body fails, whether that be years, days, or hours. I can't tell, but the pain makes me think we have less time than I'd hoped.

At least I won't have to live a second without her. When I die, she'll continue on for minutes, maybe longer, warm and protected. Then we'll leave this place forever. I'll never have to lose her. Never have to say goodbye.

I pad across the floor on already swelling feet, my hands under my bulging stomach.

Reaching down, I touch the skin between us. I hum a little, my face dewy. Glowing.

I'll carry you, Katie. Don't worry. I will carry you.

LAVENDER AND DANDELIONS

The alert goes out just after eight. Bella's finally gone down after nearly an hour of lying next to her in the dark. I scramble to silence the blaring alarm, not wanting to wake her, but as soon as the sound has ceased, I'm alone in the darkened hallway staring at my phone, the message informing me in cold, matter-of-fact language that my biggest fear has come true. The war has gone hot. There's a list of cities with the planes' known trajectories, and there's ours, halfway to the bottom. My mouth goes dry, and my tongue seems to grow too big for my mouth, gagging me. I want to scream, cry, rip out my hair, but I can't move at all. I'm frozen, rereading the warning of my impending death over and over again.

I knew it could happen. I was never in denial, and yet, it's too surreal to be believed. I force my way through the cotton-thick numbness and break my limbs from their calcified rigidity. I need to move. I need to think. Pacing up and down the hall, my footsteps are quiet on the carpet, as are Bella's soft, childish snores through her bedroom door. My phone lights up again, the siren of a warning bleating for only a second before I manage to mute it. There's an update. According to radars, the planes will be here within the hour. A link is listed beneath the update. I recognize it, no need to open it. I've been to that website dozens of times since the war began. It's the instructions for the government-issued cyanide tablets.

I think of them in the medicine cabinet, on the highest shelf where Bella couldn't reach even if she climbed up on the counter. They'd been a controversial subject, but they offered them to anyone who wanted the option. A quiet, painless end was the least they could offer their citizens. My stomach flips and I almost vomit as I visualize bursting the pills from their blister packs, placing one on Bella's tongue and one on my own, her face scrunched up with the bitter taste. No. That can't be the end.

A roaring descends on the house, shaking the walls with violent sound. I drop to the floor, cowering as I wrap my arms over my bent neck and brace myself, but after an agonizing few seconds, it passes. My legs shake, barely supporting my struggle to stand when the bedroom door cracks open and Bella's pale, terrified face appears in the darkness.

"Mommy, what was that?"

I rush to her, grabbing and lifting her as I hold her tightly to my chest, my heart beating painfully against my breastbone.

"It was just an airplane."

"It was so loud."

"I know, but it's gone now."

"I'm scared," she whimpers, and I reposition her in my arms so I can hold her better, rocking the four-year-old as if she were an infant. I close my eyes and smell her hair. Lavender shampoo, a tinge of sweat, and the slightest hint of grass stains and dandelions.

A redness spreads across my closed eyelids and my breath catches when I open my eyes and the red remains. Shades of crimson dance across the walls and carpet, illuminating the hallway. Bella wriggles to be released, and as soon as she's down, she darts to the living room where the light is pouring in. I reach out, trying to stop her, but she's too fast. She's already at the window before I'm even down the hall.

The massive picture window that I'd fallen in love with when I'd toured the house, the city skyline visible over the rolling suburban hills, is awash with distant flames, light undulating across the walls, bathing everything in vermilion. Tears roll down my cheeks as I watch the city burn.

"Pretty," Bella says, and I snap out of my silent grief, my jaw dropping open and quivering as I try to think of a way to respond. She turns to me, a timid smile on her lips.

"It looks like Christmas. No, it looks more like that time we saw the fireworks."

I nod. There's nothing else I can do. Part of me selfishly wants her to understand, to mourn the world with me, but I know it's better this way.

"Yeah, just like fireworks. Now, come on, we need to get in the car."

The smile fades from her face, leaving her eyes too dark, too big, the shadow cast on them hollowing her out. I suppress a shudder. The tension between us is palpable, and I know she feels the panic racing electric through my every nerve, urging me with excruciating pulses to *leave, leave, leave.*

"Where are we going? It's nighttime."

"Don't worry, honey. Just for a little drive. Now come on," I say, taking her arm, but she resists.

"I need Samantha."

"Fine, go grab her, quick. We've gotta go." I bite my lip as I watch her scurry to her bedroom. Every second that she's gone, the terror pulses louder in my ears, drumming the rhythm of my heart against the back of my eyes.

I can't wait any longer. I march down the hallway and find her on her knees looking under her bed.

"What's taking so long? We need to leave right now."

"I can't find her!" she sobs.

I join her in the search, tossing pillows to the floor, dropping to my own knees to peer into the darkness, digging through the overstuffed toy chest, but there's no Samantha to be found.

"I'm sorry honey, but we have to go. We'll find her when we get back," I say, and the lie tastes like ashes as it passes my lips. Bella wipes her nose on her sleeve and nods. I can't wait any longer. Picking her up again, I rush to the garage and buckle her into the booster seat. She doesn't look up at me, sniffling as tears slide down her baby face, wet strands of hair sticking to her slick face. My heart aches and I'm about to head back in to search for the doll one more time when the booming of planes overhead shakes the house so intensely that Bella covers her ears and starts to cry. No, we need to get out. Now.

I pull out of the driveway and make my way down the winding road toward the highway. Other cars pull out in front of us, driving fast and reckless, but I maneuver as defensively as I can. Neighbors gather at the tops of every hill, others stand at windows or in doorframes, mouths open and eyes aflame with the burning city.

Some houses are dark, and I can't help but imagine their bodies huddled together in beds or on sofas, foaming mouths and lifeless eyes. Perhaps they're only sleeping or left like we did. Still, I know some of them are as I imagined, waiting to be found. Maybe waiting for eternity, never found, never missed.

A shriek explodes through the night, piercing through the car despite the layers of metal and fiberglass. In the rearview mirror, I see Bella's eyes dart up, her mouth a quivering rosebud.

"Mommy, I'm scared."

"I know, honey. I'm sorry." I don't know what else to say. I have to keep going. *Leave, leave, leave.* My brainstem urges me to find a way, beat the odds, escape to safety, even when all logic tells me there's no way out. Another plane passes overhead, and an explosion over the hills shakes the car, the sky flaring red. My knuckles are blanched white as I strain to keep the steering wheel aimed straight.

"I wanna go home," Bella cries, her voice back to the way it was when she was a toddler, and I need more than anything to hold her, but I can't. We're almost to the highway. We crest the hill and I gasp, a shaking hand over my mouth.

Bumper to bumper, cars line the highway in both directions, blaring horns, trying to pass each other on shoulders, colliding and pushing each other forward with the screech of metal. They said this would happen, but my mind wouldn't accept it until now. Seeing the vehicles stretch endlessly in all directions, my pulse slows as I go numb.

I turn the car around, narrowly missing a truck that speeds past us into the mess below, taking his chance at the unmoving traffic, probably thinking he can somehow muscle his way through, but I know better.

"Bella," I say, reaching back to take her hand in mine, "it's okay. Don't cry. We'll go home. We're going home right now."

I watch in the mirror as she nods and relaxes a little. We drive past the vacant stares and weeping families on lawns as we make our way back home. A man runs to our car, bangs on the passenger window and begs for help finding his wife, but I keep my eyes on the road.

"Please! No one will help me! Please, stop and help me," the man pleas, and I watch in the mirror as he crumples in the road behind us. I swallow hard, trying to think of an appropriate explanation if Bella asks why we didn't help, but when my eyes shift to her, she's turned a sickly pale and her hands tremor at her mouth while she gnaws at her fingernails.

I pull into the garage and watch the door lower as I unbuckle Bella and take her inside. A dark drizzle has begun, staining the driveway with dark dots, slowly consuming each other until a uniform black.

"My tummy really hurts," she says, and I blink hard, trying to stop the building tears. Could it be the radiation already? The red flush of the kitchen as we walk through it reminds me that we're close enough for lethal exposure. There's no escape. There never was.

"Here, let me get you some Tylenol and that will help."

Bella watches as I pour the thick blue liquid into the cup, measuring the adult dosage of the medicine and hoping it will calm her, make her drowsy. Make it easier on her. On me.

She doesn't complain about the taste, gulping it down and handing the tiny plastic cup back to me.

"I love you, Mommy," she says, her arms darting around me, hugging me as tightly as her small body can, face buried in my shirt against my stomach. I can't answer. The impending sobs would rush out and scare her. I can only crouch down, take her in my arms, and hold her, breathing in her scent. This is what I want my last moment to be. Lavender shampoo, warm skin, grass stains, and dandelions.

"Let's go to bed. You can sleep in my bed, just like you did when you were little."

"Yay!" she says, taking my hand as I lead her to the dark bedroom, away from the flush of red and destruction. I tuck her in and tell her I'll be right back. I need to get us some more medicine for our tummies, to make sure we feel better in the morning. She nestles into the pillow, her eyelids heavy with the exhausted aftermath of terror passing.

I retrieve the pills and pop them from their packaging into my palm, but before I go back to her, I stop at her bedroom. Setting the pills on a shelf beside a porcelain rabbit and music box, I move to the bed, pull off the sheets, and shake them out. With the softest thud, a doll with yellow yarn hair and a smile of red thread falls to the carpet.

I pick up the doll and the pills, fill a glass of water, and bring them all to the bedroom. Bella is barely awake when I enter, but her eyes widen, and she smiles when I set the doll on the pillow next to her.

"You found Samantha!"

I smile, taking in every beautiful detail of the daughter I longed for all my life. The memories of the few short years together flash through my mind. Holding her swaddled in the hospital, feeding her with my breast and her happy infant gurgles and chirps. Her first birthday, the way she'd clapped and lit up when she tasted cake for the first time, and her first steps just a few weeks later. Our trips to visit my mother, trips to the zoo, afternoons at the playground, and tucking tiny dolls to sleep in her dollhouse. All I want is more. More time together. More giggles and kisses and cuddles and bedtime stories and lullabies. More Bella.

"I did. She was pushed down at the end of the bed, silly," I say, slipping under the covers next to her and pulling the quilt over us. Bella leans her head against my shoulder. I kiss her forehead. "Now it's time to take the medicine and go to sleep. Tomorrow everything will be better. It's a pill like grownups take, but it's okay to bite it. It might taste funny, but I brought some water to wash it down, and it'll help us sleep."

"Okay, Mommy," she says as I watch her take the pill and chew it, forcing it down with a grimace and then swallowing down most of the water. "Can we go to the park with the pink flower trees and the big green slide tomorrow?"

"Sure, honey. We can go wherever you want. Now let's go to sleep," I say, crushing my own pill between my teeth before washing down the bitter taste. "I love you. Goodnight."

"Goodnight," she says, draping her tiny arm over my chest, her head on my shoulder. It's only moments before I feel her fall asleep. I nestle against her, stroking her hair, sharing the same warm breath back and forth. Then I close my eyes and drift away.

GOLDEN HOUR

Sebastian follows a crab, imitating its shambling scuttle, while I press the damp sand into the plastic molds. Under my gentle guidance, he helps reveal the delicate walls and turrets.

"Let's build a moat," I say.

He digs while I fetch the water from a foam-licked wave. Walking back, I drink in every detail from the sand wedged under his short fingernails to the too-long, baby-blond ringlets I could never bring myself to cut falling into his eyes.

"Watch out, Momma! Sea monsters in the moat," he tells me, wide-eyed with pretend terror, then a roar interrupted by a giggle.

"Oh no!" I join his laughter with exaggerated surprise.

The water pours from the cup into the finger-width trench, but he juts out his hands, blocking the stream. I don't chastise him like I did when it happened. I savor the way the water dribbles over his small hands, still clinging to their infantile chubbiness.

Tears rim my eyes, but I'm smiling.

"The sun's going down." I point out the fiery oranges and reds mixing on the horizon of beating waves.

He looks past my finger and nods, cuddling into my side.

"Love you, Momma."

I take off the eyepiece then the gloves, one by one, let them fall to the floor. I don't hide them like I did those first few years, carefully coiled and pushed behind boxes. No one tries to stop me anymore.

The stairs creak under each step. I set my hand against his door. The bed is made. Toys are tidy. Dusty. How could I clean if that erases the muddy fingerprints, goldfish smashed into the carpet, skin cells and bits of hair collected in the crevices and corners?

I lay on his bed, face down on the pillow that used to smell like watermelon shampoo and childish sweat. All those scents wore away over the years, but if I try, I can make out their phantom perfume.

Breathing in everything that once was Sebastian, I ponder how to make myself live in this world. The real world. I don't belong here. I'm just a temporary visitor, to eat, drink, use the restroom, sleep a little. Then I'm back at the beach, where I should be. Watching the sunset. Making sandcastles. With him.

Everyone was patient at first, but then I lost my job. Dennis threatened to commit me, but I knew it was only empty words.

"It's not healthy," he'd say. "We've got to move on."

He left six months later. How long ago was that now? Time doesn't make sense anymore.

My sister Martha brings groceries sometimes, random things,

whatever's on sale. She knows I don't care anyway. She must pay the bills since the lights are still on and there's no eviction notice on the door.

I think about staying there. With him. I wish it was really him.

I can't move forward in life or death without him. I can't move in any direction at all.

Walk back down the stairs. Slip on the gloves, the eyepiece. Take a deep breath.

Memory selected.

Sebastian follows a crab, imitating its shambling scuttle, while I press the damp sand into the plastic molds.

WHOLE AGAIN

It happened all at once and yet stretched out across an eternity. I'd been careless. Tired. Dumb. It was a long trip back from my dad's house. I was irritable. Ready to be home. Stupid.

Cora was bouncing off the walls; it was hours past her bedtime. I remember glancing at the blue digital numbers on the car console, 11:47. I climbed out, stretched, and pumped gas, half-blinded by the harsh glaring of overhead lights, half-asleep from road hypnosis. Only an hour and a half left to get home, I told myself, talking myself out of stopping at a motel or even to pull over for a quick snooze. I had to keep going.

Cora was everything a nine-year-old can be. Obnoxious. Immature. Horrid. Hilarious. Sweet. Wonderful. She was my daughter. The love of my life and my whole world for nine years, as well as the obstacle to my personal growth, my nights off, my freedom. Being a mother was so much more complicated than

I'd imagined. I just needed her out of my hair for a minute, so without much thought, I slipped my wallet out of my purse and into her eager hands.

"Go and get yourself a snack or something."

I sent her in alone, without a second thought. I shouldn't have been surprised when she returned with her arms full, a smirk on her lips.

"What the hell, Cora?" I grabbed the three full-size bags of chips, the candy bars, and the two sodas wedged in her armpits. "Who said you could buy all this?" She shrugged and of course hadn't gotten a receipt, but still a child, she wasn't clever enough not to reveal her worst offense. From her pocket she pulled out pack after pack of those trading cards all the kids obsessed over.

"How much did you spend?"

"I don't know. Maybe twenty, thirty?"

"Cora!"

"I never get anything, and I thought it wasn't that much," her words fell out, rushed and full of remorse as I seized her shoulders, shook her, a thick shroud of rage falling over me and distorting my thoughts. Sure, it was outside our tight budget, but it wasn't the end of the world. I could cut back somewhere else to recoup the loss, and she was right that she rarely got any of the treats or surprises her friends seemed constantly showered with, but the anger clouded my mind. If I had counted to ten, it would've passed and the consequence would've waited until we got home, a grounding or a night without her phone. No, I had to blow up.

I wanted to hurt her, so in an immature overreaction, I tore open a few of the packs and scattered the cards into the crisp night air. Without a word, Cora got back in the car, slamming the door and pouting, arms crossed over her chest. I regretted it immediately, but it was too late. We hadn't gotten very far when the tire indicator came on. I cursed and she raised her eyebrows, a shadow of a smile on her lips.

"I thought we didn't say bad words, Mom?"

Slamming the door behind me, I looked at the spare and jack in the trunk and contemplated whether I even remembered how to change a tire, it'd been so long. And I was tired. So very tired. The blue of my phone illuminated my face as I tried to decide if it was worth calling AAA for help, knowing I couldn't really afford it, or if I should try on my own. Every little thing felt like a catastrophe. I was crying and screaming, kicking the flat, when Cora got out.

"Hey Mom, you look like you need help."

"Just leave me alone. I can't think," I'd snapped at her. So she did.

I can see her profile in my periphery every moment I'm awake.

She was flipping through those goddamn cards that had survived my blowup and dropped one. That was it. My sweet Cora, bent over the road when the headlights appeared; the car was moving too fast.

The sound was softer than you'd think.

Not the crack of broken bones or screams of agony, but a heavy thump and wet tearing as she was dragged, leaving behind piece after piece of herself. My ears rang with intense tinnitus. I couldn't hear my own desperate wails as I lunged after her broken body, no longer recognizable as my Cora. No longer human, she became a shredded mangle of flesh twisted in surreal positions.

The car pulled over immediately, the driver distraught, and it didn't take long for red flashing lights to illuminate the viscera that was once my daughter. They covered her with a tarp, hushing me and telling me not to look, as if I hadn't witnessed her final moments. It all blurs in my memories, a rapid, heavy heartbeat drumming in my ears over every spoken word, but there is one moment I remember clearly.

Before the driver had stepped out, before anyone noticed, I saw my baby's tiny left leg, ripped free, torn at the knee, her foot knocked from the shoe by the massive force. I can't explain why I needed that part of her. I know it makes no sense, but there was no sense to be made in those painful tragic moments.

I picked it up and tucked it in my tote before anyone could see.

My bag went unchecked, even on the long winding ride in the back of the ambulance, even by the nurses who changed me out of my blood-spattered clothing when I lost my ability to speak or move. For the rest of that night and into the next day, while I rested heavily sedated on a hospital bed, Cora's leg was in my purse across the room, barely obscured from view by the sweatshirt and yellow legal pad shoved on either side of it.

I'd forgotten I'd taken it, the entire night of the accident a haze of excruciating pain, but when I reached around for my wallet, checking out with the discharge planner, I felt it. The woman babbled on about therapy options and bereavement groups, the printer spitting out page after page of useless brochures on losing a loved one. I could only nod, mouth open, as I tried to make sense of my Cora's leg hidden in my bag. Everything was too surreal. I convinced myself I was dreaming and took a taxi home, unworried about the cost. Dream money didn't matter and soon I'd wake up.

I stared at the bag while I worked up the courage, finally summoning the strength to reach inside. I took the leg out with shaking hands, but it wasn't the gory mess I'd feared. It was Cora. A part of my beautiful, perfect Cora. My fingertips caressed it, gently wiping away the scabs of dried blood, and then I held it to my heart for the hours upon hours of heaving, choking tears.

I don't know how anyone found out about the accident, but the calls started not long after I got home. At first, I let them go to voicemail. However, I knew eventually I'd have to face someone, so when my body was left a desiccated husk, I answered, dry throat creaking and head floating with the hollow aftermath of being emptied of every sob.

"Don't worry about a thing. I've got it covered," my brother Tyler told me. "But I have to ask, did you have Cora covered by any life insurance? I'm sorry, but it'd certainly help with the costs and everything."

When my phone finally quieted, partially because it was late at night and partially because I'd given up and switched it over to "do not disturb," I found a new wave of grief waiting for me. I held her bare foot to my cheek until I fell asleep, whimpering on the couch.

In the morning, I had a little more clarity. Before I took a double dose of the tranquilizers the hospital had given me and curled into my damp corner of the couch, stained with tears and sweat from nightmares, I had to find a place to put Cora's leg.

I was scared for anyone to find it, though I couldn't pinpoint why. Was I afraid they'd find me disgusting, morbid, perverse for keeping it? Or was it that they'd take her away from me, this last spoiling piece of her, everything else collected and kept away already? It certainly wasn't a fear of being locked away in a psychiatric hospital, though I was sure that would happen as well. I didn't really care about living anymore. I would've taken myself out, to meet either Cora again or enter an endless unfeeling void, neither option unappealing, but I didn't have the strength. Not even enough energy to kill myself; it was honestly so absurd I could've laughed, but I didn't. There was no more laughter, no more tears, nothing except sleep, Cora's leg carefully wrapped up and hidden in the back of the refrigerator. It pained me to put it away, having to treat it as the piece of flesh it was, but I didn't want it to decompose. I couldn't bear that.

As the next few days passed by and preparations were made, I was surprised no one noted the leg's absence. Didn't they wonder where this part of my child had gone? That was until the devastating reality hit me like a punch to the gut: she'd been so destroyed by the accident that they likely couldn't take any accurate survey of her parts. My poor child, the love of my life, had been scraped off the asphalt with a shovel. I wanted to erase the image of her spread thin down the patch of road, but it came back again and again.

When the funeral finally came, it was a mandatory closed casket. I remember the funeral director telling me it was better I didn't see, as if I hadn't seen already. I wanted to look, as horrible as it'd be, to make sure it was my Cora inside, but they'd sealed the casket shut. I picked at the seal with a fingernail as I leaned over the pearly pink veneer and whispered my apologies into the cold steel. My brother had chosen pink because I'd been too deep in my grief to help. I winced to imagine her buried forever in her most hated color, but there was nothing to be done.

At least she didn't have to see it, I thought, and my skin burst into a flurry of goosebumps to imagine the busted sack of organs that was once my daughter buried under suffocating layers of dirt and dark and squirming insects. I tried to get away before the vomit escaped my lips, only making it a few steps from the casket. Everyone said they understood, helping me to a chair, wiping my chin and dabbing at my dress. They were so gentle with me, as if I'd break into a thousand ceramic pieces with the slightest touch. I'd even ruined her funeral.

When I got home, Dad, Tyler, and a few others stayed with me for a while, probably until they deemed it socially acceptable to leave. Then I was alone. I hated their company, their awkward condolences and tiptoed chitchat, but as soon as they were gone, I missed the distraction. I couldn't help myself, praying for forgiveness as I took the leg out and warmed its chilled flesh against my skin. Beneath the coppery scent of blood, it still smelled like her. Grapefruit body wash and the sweet smell of childish sweat.

How could she be gone?

Before I took the nightly handful of pills to keep me numb and help me sleep, I tucked the leg under my pillow, my hand resting against the downy hairs and smooth skin as I drifted away. All night I dreamt of Cora, watching her whole life all over again. When I woke in the late morning, I stayed huddled under the blankets for a long time. I knew I had to do something with the leg before long. It wasn't respectful to her memory to keep it until it rotted. I needed to bury it or cremate it, a private goodbye to my daughter, and yet I couldn't get myself out of bed to start the day. I wanted every moment possible with the last piece of her left.

Bare feet dug into the carpet. I held my breath as I removed the pillow, gently as if Cora could still feel, as if I could hurt her if I moved too fast. And there it was.

It took me a moment to fully comprehend what I was seeing. The same tiny toes, same arched foot, same soft blonde-haired calf, same knobby knee, but where the thigh was ripped away, there was no longer a dried, ragged stump and shredded skin. Instead, a bulb of pristine new flesh had appeared over the top.

I gasped, staggered backward, and hit my back against the wall. It made no sense, but I could only gape in silence for so long. My hands tremored as I reached out, gently touching the skin. I darted back, breathing hard. It was warm.

My mind grasped for any logical explanation, and I realized perhaps my own body heat had warmed it during the night. Significantly calmed down, I touched it again. It was very warm and as my fingers traveled up the shin bone and over the bulbous growth, I felt the contracting of muscles and the ripple of movement. I brushed my nails over the sole of the foot, and the toes wriggled as if the nerve endings were stimulated. Cora had always been ticklish, even as a baby.

When I held the leg to me this time, fresh tears streamed down my cheeks and neck, collecting at my chest where I pressed it, and the leg seemed to hug back. My Cora. She wasn't fully gone.

Every night, I slept with the leg tucked in next to me, wrapped in my daughter's favorite plush blanket and with her toy otter swaddled in with her, and every day, I spent time researching strange and supernatural phenomenon on the internet, hoping to find something like this. There was never anything like it, only an obvious hoax or two.

Over the week, I watched the lump of flesh lengthen into a cylinder until it had formed a full thigh, exactly like Cora's down to the twin moles just below her hip. In another week, she consisted of a full pelvis, a soft belly, and the start of another thigh. There was no need for explanation. Cora was coming back to me.

With my bereavement leave up, I started getting calls from work, but I ignored them. I didn't bother going to any of the follow-up therapy sessions or to refill my prescriptions. I didn't answer any texts or calls from friends or family either. They wouldn't understand why I wasn't sad anymore. How could I explain the miracle that was happening slowly right before my eyes?

Two more weeks and I'd dipped into my savings account to pay the rent and grocery deliveries. I didn't dare leave the house. Cora couldn't be alone. Not yet. She was fully formed to the clavicle, with two perfect arms and two perfect legs. At night, she held me in her arms, though they were weak and still fell limp occasionally. I'd rest my head against her chest, listening to the strong thrumming of her heart.

I had so many questions that needed answers. Was she hungry? I'd hear her stomach rumble but had no way of providing nourishment unless I could get an IV, which I would have somehow obtained if needed; however she continued to grow without it. Using a blood pressure cuff that Dad left over long ago, I found her to be perfectly within the normal range, so she couldn't be dehydrated or suffering. It was a genuine miracle. One I didn't deserve.

When her neck sprouted, I was giddy at the idea of hearing her sweet voice again. When her jaw appeared, I counted the lovely teeth and coated her tongue with sponged water, moisturized her lips with a thin layer of lip balm. My job finally terminated me, leaving a voicemail and sending a letter by mail. They sounded concerned beneath the frustrated professionalism, but it was necessary I stay home. Now that she was drinking, she needed me to walk her blind healing body to the toilet, to dress her, to keep her nourished, to make sure she was taken care of.

Cheeks formed, a maxilla and nose, but she still didn't talk. I kissed the half-face, nuzzling her nose like I did when she was an infant. I felt like a new mother again, reliving those all-encompassing first months when Cora needed all my time and patience. She began to eat soft, easy-to-swallow foods. I was terrified she would choke, so I watched her carefully, giving her the full attention she deserved. She began to stagger around the house on her own, using her outstretched arms and open palms, as one walks through a darkened unfamiliar house. But I was sure soon she'd remember. Soon she'd see.

With the sprouting of lovely ears, so delicate, their attached lobes just like I remembered, I could whisper my apologies and eternal love and a million promises of how I'd be a better mom this time around. How thankful I was that she was coming back to me.

I would never put work first again, no matter how badly we needed the money. I wouldn't miss another day with her. I'd be a witness to every milestone, a helping hand through every hardship. I'd do anything for her. I could never make up for the tired, stupid, shitty parent I had been before, but I could try.

When I woke up after three days of stunted progress, I gasped, tracing my fingers down her apple cheeks. Her eyelids fluttered open, and she looked at me. Her skull was fully formed, fused, the fuzz of new growth scattered across her scalp.

"Cora, I—I love you. I'm so sorry." The words poured out of me in deep braying sobs until she stopped me with a finger on my lips. She didn't talk and still struggled to walk, but my daughter was back.

By the afternoon, a bit of the astonishment had worn off and I was formulating how I might reintroduce her to the world. Cora had died according to the paperwork and eyewitnesses. Would they accuse me of fraud? Would they take her away to conduct experiments? My blood stilled at the thought. I'd never let that happen. Maybe a few close, trustworthy loved ones needed to know for now. Tyler, even though he was sometimes an asshole big brother, was the first who came to mind, and a slight shame washed over me as I remembered my phone. I hadn't even charged it in over a week, leaving it a black dead screen on the kitchen counter. Just as I'd plugged it in, there was a loud, frantic rapping at the door.

"Hello? Please let me in. I'm worried about you."

It was Tyler. I looked at Cora, her eyes full of confusion and fear, and I froze until he added, "If you don't let me in, I'm going to call the cops or bust down this door. Please don't be dead in there."

The anxious hurt in his voice was too much. I tried to reassure myself that I trusted him as I kissed Cora's forehead and went to the door. I opened it a crack and watched the relief spread over his features, his brow smoothing and eyes misting up.

"God, you scared the hell outta me. Why have you been ignoring me?"

"I've had some things I needed to work through alone, that's all." The blush crept over my face, deep and burning with shame.

"I know losing Cora has been incredibly difficult for you, but the answer isn't to shut everyone out." Tyler sighed, shifting his weight awkwardly. "I went to your work first. They said you just never answered them again and they had to let you go."

"Listen, I had a good reason. It'll all make sense in a minute." I took a deep breath. "Come inside. There's something I need to show you."

I saw his eyes dart to the half-hidden smile on my lips and his face faded two shades paler, but when I opened the door and walked toward the kitchen, he followed.

Cora was still sitting in her usual place, pushing scrambled eggs around her plate with a fork. A sniffled combination of a laugh and a sob accompanied the grin I could no longer contain. I turned to Tyler, ready to explain, but the way his face had gone haggard and sickly made me stumble on my words.

"What the fuck? Is that—is that what I think it is?" His eyes rolled wildly to me, the whites showing all around and venom striking me with every word. I wheeled back to the table, but she wasn't there.

"Cora!" I screamed, looking around the room, running to her chair and pulling it out, as if she might've shrunk and hidden under the table. Then I saw it.

On the table was Cora's leg. Only the foot, calf, and knee with the jagged tear where it had been shorn from her fragile body, but it was worse than before. The skin was shriveled, discolored with patches of dark rot and bits of furry mold. A distinct smell, sharp like cheese and rancid, wafted from where the leg lay, but that didn't stop me from grabbing it and holding it to my chest again.

She was still my daughter.

"What did you do?" I shrieked, turning to Tyler, my vision blacking to a pinpoint of pounding light aimed right at his face.

"What do you mean?"

"She was here! She had healed. Come back Cora!" I fell to my knees. "You ruined everything by coming here!"

I heard his footsteps, quick and heavy out of the house, and his voice far away, telling someone my address and the nature of his emergency. I didn't look up. In my arms, I cradled the last part of Cora, kissing the kneecap gently as I rocked her back and forth. They'd never understand. She just needed more time. I knew what I needed to do, take the pills, all of them, and sleep with her in my arms until she grew back again. That was all we needed. A long rest together. She'd come back. She had to, so I could apologize again and finally hear her answer: that she forgives me.

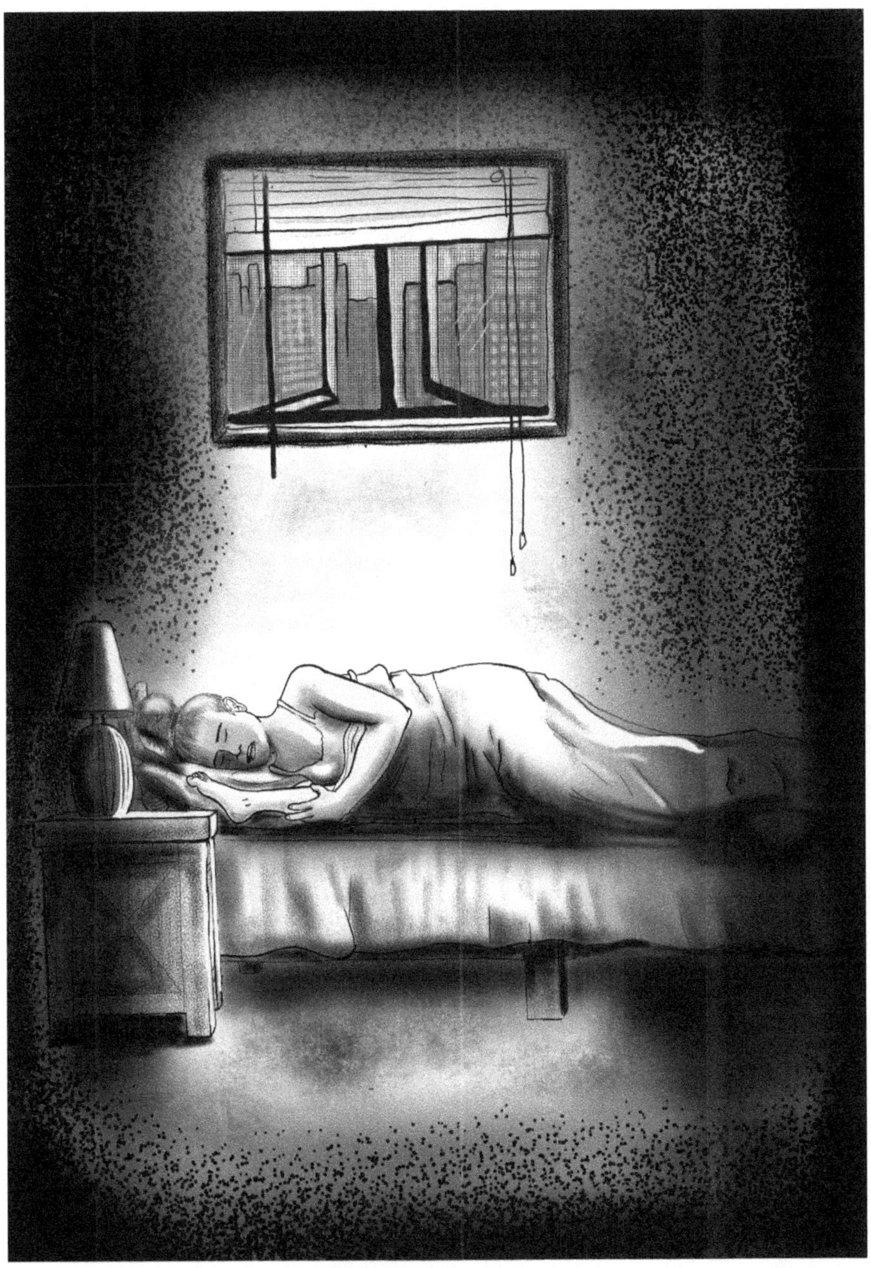

A BETTER MOTHER

Her hand slides across her rotund belly as she examines the yellow terry cloth onesie. An absent-minded smile graces her lips as she searches the rest of the rack. Her long fingers constantly tap the top of her stomach, an annoying habit of hers that makes me feel like yelling, "How would you feel if someone was always tapping on the roof of your home, not letting you sleep? Doesn't he kick in protest? Don't you want him to sleep peacefully?" But I restrain myself.

No, no. Deep calming breaths. There you go. No need to blow your top at her. She's just a young mother, definitely a first timer. Without thinking, my hand slides down my own protruding belly and I let out a slow exhale. The anger flows out, through my feet, into the floor. Breathe with intention. Calm steady breaths. Don't want to spike my blood pressure. There we go.

She still hasn't noticed I'm watching her, oblivious little thing that she is. That's alright, I don't mind waiting a bit. She might not know it yet, but I'm just the woman she needs in her life. Someone who knows the ropes of motherhood. Someone to take her under their wing, who can unburden her of the guilt and naïveté that nearly crushes her like a lost baby fawn. I sneer. She's really quite pathetic.

Meandering through the clothing racks and cutesy displays, I follow her and wait for the inevitable doubt. That nagging feeling all first-time mothers feel deep down in their gut, questioning every choice from the important to the mundane to the absolutely stupid. A sincere moment of weakness. Will this rabbit rattle be entertaining enough for my infant? Would they rather have the green onesie with the frog or the yellow one with the lion? Give me a break. I smirk down at my stomach and remember when I was just like her, all those years ago. Thank God I know better now.

She slips down the next aisle, but I'm already backtracking, making sure I'm close enough to observe without alerting her. Then, there it is. My heart leaps. There's the look. A twinge of guilt mixed with a barely discernible dampening to the eyes, not enough to push even one tear out, but I see it. Her shopping cart swivels to the side, and she stops. There's a quiver at her lips, her brows knitting tightly together as she looks at the car seat, the price tag sliding between her fingers. She wants it. She *needs* it. I watch the desolate look wash over her face. That's when I make my move.

"Hey, good choice! That's an excellent car seat. I had one just like it with my last one." I calculate my voice to be simultaneously affable and authoritative. That's what works best with her type, the uneasy, insecure first timers. Predictably, her head snaps up and her eyes widen to take me in, a protective hand darting to her belly. The defensive pose lasts only a second before she registers me as another one of her kind: pregnant, safe, perhaps a little lonely. She laughs in a tinny, relieved way that grates on my ears, but I don't let on.

"Oh, you startled me," she says, another laugh followed by an embarrassed sigh. "Yeah, this one looks really good, but it's a little pricey. At least for right now. Maybe by the time the next one comes along," she shrugs and forces out another laugh. Then again with that tap, tap, *tapping* of fingers across her belly. Why won't she stop doing that! I can't help myself, a microsecond of a scowl creeping up as I glance down to her stomach and then back to her face. I wasn't fast enough. She stills her hand nervously.

Come on now, not too aggressive, I warn myself. Don't want to scare her off.

"It's well worth the price. I'm telling you, the way it can detach and then plug right into the matching stroller, such a lifesaver."

"I'm sorry, do you work here?" She looks at me, then past me down the aisle, as if she expects some uniformed manager to be watching us, nudging me along to make a sale. A tight, polite smile crinkles my nose.

"Nope. Sorry if I'm a bother. Just seeing you with this one brought back memories of my first and how many times I lugged that thing into doctor appointments and over to my mom's house. Was just a bit nostalgic, I guess. Well, you have a good day, sweetheart." The last word oozes out in my most matronly, warm tone and her shoulders fall, relaxing under the slight intoxication of motherly attention. Yes, my dear. That's the way.

I reach out, lightly touching her arm. Her skin is burning hot, even through the thin cardigan. She looks to my hand and then to my face and doesn't pull away. She feels she can trust me. My smile relaxes. I've succeeded.

"No, you're no bother at all. It's just, if I could afford something as nice as this car seat, I'd certainly get it." I see her glance at the unnecessary items in her cart: a couple outfits, a black and white patterned mobile, a few pacifiers. "Maybe I'll put it on my registry." She laughs an easy laugh, like we've become instant good friends. "Can you believe I haven't had my baby shower yet? Guess my momma's waiting till the last minute." Her fingers tap across her belly again. I try my best to ignore it. "Hope she gets to it soon or else the baby'll be here."

"Yeah, nobody's thrown me one yet either. I guess they don't do very much for a second," I say, carefully painting on a bashful smile. "If you don't mind my asking, how many weeks are you? Looks like you're heading into the home stretch."

"Oh yeah, almost there. Just hit 37 weeks yesterday. How about you?"

"I'm right behind you at 35 weeks. Getting close now. I bet you're ready for the torture of all this to be over, right?" I laugh and pat my stomach, but gently, not like her sharp tapping claws. Maybe she'll learn by example.

"I mean, it's not easy but I wouldn't call it *torture*. That's a bit extreme," she says with a light, fake laugh, and takes a half step back. I feel my forehead start to furrow but I force my face back into the smooth, jovial, fellow mom-to-be I need her to see. I want to slap myself for my foolish word choice. They can be so sensitive. That's what cost me in the past. She crosses her arms as I take a small step forward.

"You're right, I wouldn't call it torture either. I think I'm just a little moody from this little guy not letting me sleep last night, what with the heartburn, back aches, constant restroom breaks, plus his midnight gymnastics." I watch her shoulders lower along with her guard. "Just wait till you get to your second one. Honey, it is so much harder the second time around, especially if you're a bit older like me." I take the risk and reach out, touch her shoulder. Her eyes lock with mine and I feel her soften.

"I'm sure. How old is your other one?" Her arms uncross. Her stance relaxes.

"Gabrielle is seven. Oh my gosh, no, almost eight! So it's been a while since I've had to go through all this. I remembered it being easier," I laugh heartily again, and she joins me, only a little apprehensive. "They grow up so fast. I'm Ashley by the way."

I offer my hand and she obliges, making sure I shake it firmly, and holding onto it just a little longer than normal, forcing her to continue the social story I've set in action.

"I'm Caitlin. Well, I guess I should be going. Most of this stuff's a little out of my price range anyway."

She smiles politely and moves toward her cart, but I reach out to stop her, nice and gentle on the arm like before.

"You know, I've actually been thinking about replacing my old car seat. Hell, the stroller too. Car seats go through a lot before a baby outgrows 'em, if you know what I mean. How'd you like to take the old one off my hands? For free, of course. My husband's making plenty lately; I don't have to worry about pinching pennies like I used to, with the first one."

I gesture toward her and she blushes slightly. I see the discomfort bubbling up inside her and she stammers a little before I cut her off. "Oh, I'm sorry! I hope you don't find this incredibly rude! I didn't mean anything by it. I just remember what it was like is all. I was in a real rough spot with my first one, and I only wanted to help if I could. Don't worry 'bout a thing, sweetheart."

And just like that, all her misgivings melt away as she realizes what she might be losing out on. I know as well as she does that she could never afford that fancy car seat, let alone the stroller combo, so she can't let this deal walk away, even if it is from some pretentious middle-aged moneybags like me.

"Wow, uh, I can't believe you'd just give it away to a stranger like that—"

I cut her off. "I know it seems weird, but—" I force a dramatic heavy sigh and drop my voice a little closer to a whisper. "I've been in your place, honey. I can see it in your face. Times were tough when Gabrielle came, and I'd just like to pay it forward. Do something good for once."

It works so well, tears start welling up in her eyes. In no time, I've convinced her to follow me to my place where she can pick up the car seat and stroller, as well as some other baby odds and ends. I barely tear my eyes away from the rearview mirror the whole drive home, anticipating her intuition to kick in. I'm sure I'll watch her turn around and race away at any second, but she doesn't.

As I pull into the driveway, I see her park at the curb and she's biting her lips. The hesitation is palpable from across the yard. Dammit. I came across too strange. I consider walking toward her, but my gut tells me it'd seem more realistic, and a little less uncanny, if I just walk to my door like anyone would. It's the right call. Her car door shuts and I don't turn around until I've unlocked the door and hear her high heels tapping up behind me. I still can't believe this nitwit: wearing pumps in her third trimester? Ridiculous.

"Come on in, the baby stuff's all in the garage. I know, I know. It's so close and I haven't even gotten around to pulling out more than the freaking crib. I really need to get moving on that." I drop my keys onto a pile of laundry on the coffee table. "Hope you don't mind the mess, by the way. Sorry for that. I'm not the best housekeeper." I laugh, but I never take my eyes off her. She's still skittering around, nervous as a rabbit.

"Can I use your bathroom? He's bouncin' on my bladder again," she asks, grinning and pointing at her stomach, her hand shaking just slightly. I nod and restrain my disgust this time. She knows something is off. Her instincts must be whispering to her. Gotta keep it cool.

"Sure. Of course. I know how that is. It's just down this hall, second door on the left. Go on ahead, dear."

As she waddles down the corridor, I take my time, flipping every lock on the front door, smoothing back my hair into a ponytail, and finally, sliding the claw hammer out from the pile of clothes on the sofa. The wood handle warms in my tight grasp, becoming an extension of myself. Everything feels perfect. Then

I wait. And wait. And why is she taking so damn long?

I slip the hammer into my back pocket, where it hangs awkward and ready to rip the pocket off, and peek down the hall. The bathroom door is still shut, light on.

"Are you okay?" I shout down the hall. She doesn't respond. Then I notice Gabrielle's bedroom door is cracked open. Bounding down the hall, hand on the hammer, I get to the room just as she opens the door.

"What are you doing in there? I thought you had to go piss," I hiss through clenched teeth, my face contorted in a deep scowl for just a second before I realize and smooth it back to placid neutrality. Don't have much time now.

"I'm sorry, I just—this is your daughter's room? Danielle, right? When does she come home from school? Must be any minute now I bet."

"Gabrielle. And no. School doesn't let out for another couple hours and then she's gotta ride the bus all the way here. Don't worry, we have plenty of time to load up your car with all the goodies. Come on over here, like I said, it's all in the garage."

"You know, I'm feeling guilty about the whole thing. I mean, what if you change your mind or something?" She starts to babble, the words flowing out faster and faster, all the while tapping away at her stomach again like a goddamn keyboard. "I think I should just give you a few days to think it over and make sure for real. I can give you my email and you can let me know, then we could meet at the store again and—"

Holding the hammer up, my lower lip quivering, I slowly reiterate my instructions. "We are going to the garage *now*." She nods just as slowly. I walk around behind her, hammer hovering near her skull, then I lower it, prodding her toward the garage door.

Those clinking heels of hers are now light as a cat, making small, hesitant steps across the carpet in front of me. My cheeks and face burn and I feel like screaming, rushing her over there, but deep controlled breaths are key. I'm in charge now. Just a few more steps.

She bolts toward the front door. I swing out instinctively and miss, almost falling with the momentum. I can't believe how fast she's moving, sprinting across the room in those fucking heels. The dumb bitch is at the door, one lock undone, two undone, then struggling with the chain. That's just enough time and I'm there, body slamming her against the door. I hear her hand crack against the metal lock, and she shrieks before I grab her and pull her around to face me.

My hand shoots up to cover her mouth. Her lips snarl, teeth tearing into my palm. She tries to bite my hand again, but I brandish the hammer and she stops. Her eyes widen and lock with mine while her tears and snot flow down the back of my hand. Shaking uncontrollably, her hands clasp around my own, covering her mouth, and she gently pushes at it.

"Don't you dare fucking scream. Don't try a fucking thing," I whisper and release her mouth, keeping the hammer hovering near her head.

"You don't want to do this. Listen to me. Please. I'm begging you. You don't want to hurt me!" Her voice starts to raise but she quickly controls it again. "What about your own baby? And your daughter, she needs you. They need you. Please." As hard as she tries to keep control, the words dissolve into sobs, trails of snot running from her nostrils into her mouth. "Why are you doing this?"

"You don't deserve that little fucking miracle inside you. You know that? With all your goddamn tapping and look at those heels, a fucking tripping hazard, and something you shouldn't have wasted your money on with a baby on the way. I doubt you even have a daddy for that baby. Look at you, you live at home with your momma, letting her work her ass off to take care of you while you just leech off society. Don't try to tell me different. I know your type. You don't deserve any of it. You're a fucking trainwreck and yet you, *you* get to have a wonderful, precious little angel. No, no, no. God made a mistake but now I'm correcting it. He sent you to me so I could correct it. I'm the better mother. I deserve this."

I watch as the horror settles over her. All color drains from her face, and her mouth droops open just a bit, her knees starting to buckle. I can't help but smile, knowing soon that little one will be crying in my arms. *My baby. It's meant to be mine.* Suddenly, she shoves me in the belly, her hands pushing deep into the padding, and she's scurrying past me.

I try to regain my balance but fall to my knees, jerking my head in time to see her trying the back door, pushing and pulling, but she can't figure it out. I start to laugh as I get up and head towards her, hammer in hand.

She sees me and gives up on the door, heading into the kitchen. Dead end. Then rushing toward me before rapidly turning left, wrenching open the door and heading right into the garage, pulling the door shut behind her, but it's no use. There's no lock there. I take a deep breath and follow her inside.

Just as I'd guessed, she's tugging at the garage door, trying to pull it up. Her eyes dart wildly as she stops every few seconds to look around the room. Her hands scramble around the door frame, looking for something. Probably for some sort of emergency release. Does she really think I didn't consider these things? That I didn't prepare for all possibilities?

I straighten my back, pushing out my padded stomach and breasts and carefully approach her, hammer held high. She tries to dart away, but this time I bring it down and feel the sharp crack and the hot blood splatters across my face. I catch a glance of her face as she falls. Life dims then extinguishes in that final second we share, eyes locked.

The body lands at my feet with a soft thud. I take my time, first removing my padding to give myself more flexibility and then taking out the iodine, scalpel, retractors, and gauze. Remembering the medical books I've read over and over at the library, step by step, I cut through each delicate layer, trying to be quick yet thorough. I know time is of the essence. As the muscle fights me, often tearing and ripping inaccurately, I curse at how much more difficult this is than I'd imagined. Even the dog I'd practiced on was easier than this. At least I don't have to worry about stitching her back together when I'm through. As long as I'm careful of the baby, that's all that matters.

Finally, I hack my way through the last bands of muscle and find the soft membrane I've been searching for. Floating peacefully unaware in the amniotic fluid, there is my little one. My fingers press against the fragile barrier between us, grazing the back of the curled hand.

"I'm here to save you. Mommy is here," I whisper.

The sack breaks with a gush of warm fluid under my scalpel. My hands dart in, catching the child and bringing him out into the cold world. It shivers as I quickly cut through the dense tissue of the umbilical cord before tossing the blade away. I look at the child for a moment, taking in every beautiful detail before pressing him to my chest, trying to warm him.

It's a boy, just like I'd foreseen. Just like my own little one should've been, had he made it this far. The baby squirms silently. He's still alive. Sobs shudder out from between my lips and clenched teeth. Please stay alive. Lord, have mercy on him.

My hands cradle him as I pull him from her wretched womb, gently pouring sterile water over him and wiping at his face with a washcloth. Suddenly, his tiny mouth stretches wide, and he begins to cry. I'm holding him to my breast when I hear the door open behind me.

"Did the baby come?" Gabrielle's timid voice echoes to me across the garage.

"Oh honey, your brother is here. Your brother is finally—" but I can't finish as the sobs overtake me.

II

TAKE CONTROL

As Sara swung open the door to the parking garage, the roaring noise of the storm and the chill in the air surrounded the two young girls. Her little sister Kiara shivered and rubbed her arms as she followed Sara around the corner to the ramp leading down to the third floor. Water cascaded down the sides of the structure, the few cars empty and waiting on a Wednesday afternoon, their dark windshields facing out toward the rain. Sara nearly had to shout to be heard above the din.

"You get to try first since it was your present, but don't hog it."

She set the large toy jeep on the concrete and reluctantly passed the remote to her sister's eager hands. Kiara's entire face beamed with pride as she tried the controls and watched the purple vehicle lurch forward then backward at her command.

"Be careful now," Sara warned, reaching out as if to take the controller, but Kiara twisted away. Her thumb orchestrated a sharp turn, almost flipping the toy car.

"I got it! I got it!" she shouted, furrowing her brow, and twisting further away from her sister. Concentrating on the tiny joysticks, the tip of her tongue stuck out from her lips.

"Careful or you're gonna crash!" Sara shouted, grabbing for the controller again.

"No, I've got it. See?"

Kiara guided the jeep in a perfect figure eight before bringing it back to stop at their feet. With a smirk and sidelong glance before quickly bursting into giggles, the five-year-old handed the controller to her sister as if challenging her to prove the supposed superiority she pretended three years gave her.

"Now watch this," Sara said, right away pushing the joystick as hard as she could so that the little car skidded then roared full throttle back down the ramp. Suddenly, she lost control and Kiara started screaming in her ear. Her mind glaze with panic as her shaky hands attempted to steer. She over-corrected and the jeep dramatically flipped over and over again before landing on its wheels and careening around the corner, stopping out of view with a loud crash.

Both girls gasped as the color ran from their faces. Kiara started to whimper, her bottom lip jutting out and quivering as tears spilled down her cheeks.

"Don't cry. I bet it's not too bad. Let's go see," Sara said, trying to be brave for her little sister, but holding her breath as they made their way down the ramp, almost too afraid to look.

There it was: the purple paint scratched, wheels still whirring, and resting on its side next to the fresh dent along the door of a minivan.

"Momma's gonna kill us," Kiara whispered, eyes wide and fixed on the wreck.

"Naw, she'll never know," Sara answered as she picked up the jeep and righted it.

"But look, there's even a little purple on the van! Momma is gonna kill us for sure."

The kindergartner burst into tears, but her big sister ignored her except for a cursory hush as she squatted next to the dented door and attempted to scratch away the few telltale purple flakes with the bitten nubs of her fingernails.

"There, look. There's no way anyone will know it was us now. You can stop crying."

"Momma told us we weren't allowed to play without her watching, and now she's gonna find out and take it away and I've barely even gotten to play with it at all," the girl said, interrupting herself with sobs every couple words.

"I told you; she'll never know!" Sara shouted, but as soon as the words left her lips, she got a strange feeling and the air caught in her lungs and throat, ice cold. Her mouth dropped open a tiny bit as her eyes scanned the shadows and empty cars for whoever she could feel watching them. Finally, she found him.

A pasty-skinned man with square, dark-rimmed glasses watched the girls from behind the wheel of a scuffed-up, light blue Mercedes. His face was almost expressionless, like a mannequin, but his dark eyes burned into Sara's and made her stomach squirm. The car sat dark, parked between two unoccupied vehicles, six or so cars down the line. The man watched them, half hidden in shadow and barely blinking.

Kiara sensed her sister's unease and stopped crying, sniffling a little as she looked around before also catching sight of the strange man. His gaze slowly shifted from the eldest girl to the younger one, and for a moment, they both stared back, hypnotized by fear.

Sara finally broke free and picked up the jeep, cradling it in her arms, then turned away so she wouldn't feel compelled to look any longer.

"Let's go up to the top and play."

Kiara whimpered again. "But that guy saw us hit the car. He's gonna tell on us."

"No, he won't. He's just some weirdo. Come on, let's go."

"I've never seen a guy like that before. He's staring at us."

"I know," Sara growled, hugging the car tightly to her chest with one arm while the other yanked her sister along. "He's freaking me out. Let's go."

"What's wrong with him?"

"Probably just drugs, like Momma always says."

"I wanna go home."

"No, not yet. Momma's gonna know we snuck out the second she hears that door, and you know you're gonna step on the creaky spot like always. Don't you want to play with your car just a little more before she takes it away?"

"Fine," Kiara said, biting her lip and bowing her head slightly as they walked.

The wind howled and blew chilly raindrops through the

parking garage as they walked up the ramp, then the next, and the next until they reached the top of the building where the roof ended, opening to the swirling grey sky. Only a few cars were left in the storm on the exposed roof, the rain mixing with small hail that bounced up from the concrete and made tinny noises as it collected on the hoods and windshields.

Sara set the toy car down as the girls huddled together near the top of the ramp, just far enough from the opening to stay dry. She drove it out onto the roof, splashing through a puddle, but then noticed Kiara's teary eyes, and with a sigh, handed the controller back to her sister.

They laughed and cheered each other on, passing the controller back and forth as they took turns racing the jeep around the roof of the parking garage until that same uneasy feeling came over Sara and she compulsively turned around.

The car with the waxy, pale man had soundlessly creeped behind them at some point over the last ten minutes, parking in the middle of the lanes, facing them. The man was standing outside the driver side door, watching them. He was a little taller than average and his pallid face and black frames of his glasses made the dark irises of his eyes even more prominent. He wore casual clothing, nothing unusual: jeans, a faded blue tee with a red and orange bird spread across the chest, and a black baseball cap, but there was something unnerving about his appearance she couldn't pinpoint. She tried to brush the thought away, but everything about the man caused a feeling of pulsing red alarm to flash through her mind.

Kiara instantly felt her sister stiffen. She turned around and gasped. She dropped the controller but quickly bent over and picked it up, looking to the man, then her sister, then back to the man again. She felt the sobs building inside her, but she kept them contained as she looked to Sara to cue their next move. The jeep sat idle behind them while hail and hard rain pummeled it.

"I saw what happened downstairs," the man said, his voice slow and sugary like sickening molasses, though loud enough to hear over the storm. He clicked his tongue and shook his head with displeasure.

"It was just an accident, mister. No big deal." Sara spoke in a nonchalant, calm voice, but inside her heart quaked in her chest.

"Ah, no big deal. No big deal? I bet the family who owns that van wouldn't think it was 'no big deal.'"

"Sure, they would. There was hardly a dent. Now would you please leave us—"

"Oh really? Do you know the family that drives that car?"

"No, sir," Kiara muttered, holding her hands together in front of her, eyes downcast and face darkening. Sara nudged her with an elbow.

"No, we don't, but we will write them a sorry letter and leave it on the car. I'm sure they won't—"

"A sorry note? Heh, I'm sure your mom would want you to do more than that. Oh buddy, she's going to be mad at y'all."

"No, she won't," Sara snapped, but Kiara was already nodding and crying.

"You girls better come with me so we can all go tell her."

Kiara's cries intensified, becoming audible even above the crashing rain. A shiver ran down Sara's spine, and she felt like she was breathing deeper and faster than before; her eyes taking in every detail around her, and yet they all became jumbled in her frenzied thoughts.

"What do you mean? You don't know our mom. You need to leave us alone right now!" She spat the words out like venom, her upper lip rising a little as she finished.

"I do know your mom, and I'm also a police officer so I have a duty to report your accident. Even if it was a toy car, you still caused damage so there has to be a report. So now, come along."

An ancient instinct made Sara put her arm up against her sister and step back, forcing the sobbing girl a few paces back with her.

"You don't look like a cop, and you definitely don't know our mom. You need to go away right now or…or…I'll scream."

The man took two steps toward them, closing the distance she had created. He seemed calm, though he moved his lips together like he was hiding his agitation.

"I don't want you to start screaming because there's no reason for that. I'm a cop and I'm just here to help the poor owner of that van. But if you did scream, it wouldn't matter…the rain'll drown it out. And if it doesn't, no one will hear you anyway, or they'd just think you're screaming while you're playing." He half smirked before his face smoothed back into an expressionless mask.

"Not if I scream for help," Sara said, but the man stood just as relaxed and blank as ever.

Sara's heart pounded like a drum in her throat as she realized he was right. She pushed Kiara back another few steps with her until they felt the rain splattering on their hair and backs, almost out from under the overhang.

The pale man moved back toward his car, opened the door, and bent over. The trunk clicked as the lock released. The man walked behind the car, opening the trunk just a little before slamming it closed again. He came back to the door and bent to reach inside, as if collecting something from the cupholder or passenger seat.

For just a second, Sara let herself believe he might leave, but he straightened again and returned his piercing gaze at the girls. She hated herself for not taking the opportunity to run for help. She tried to move her feet, but they felt heavy and dull. Kiara sobbed quietly by her side.

The man walked toward them again, stepping in front of his car, and Sara's pulse raced as the tire iron came into view from behind his leg, his left hand clutching the handle.

"Why do you have that?" she asked, but much too softly for him to hear over the rain. She didn't need him to answer.

Next to her, Kiara's cries stifled, and Sara looked over to see her sister's mouth gaping, bottom lip quivering, and eyes opened so wide the white showed all around. Then her eyes snapped shut, looking small and tight in her face as her mouth opened in another howling wail.

She glanced back to the man who wielded the tire iron, a simple tool now posing an ominous threat she'd never thought of before. He bounced it gently in his hand, passed it between his palms, then bounced it again as if weighing it, his own eyes caressing the tool with an almost loving gaze.

Sara's stomach tightened and twisted. She breathed in quick, shallow breaths, feeling like she couldn't get enough air. Her vision blurred in and out as her mind swam, lightheaded. Kiara's cries continued next to her, making it hard to think. Swallowing, trying to retain composure, Sara swayed on her unsteady legs and silently prayed for a miracle: take us away, anywhere but here.

"Shut up! Won't you shut her up?" the man's whispered shout hissed through the roar of the wind. He took a few jerking, almost lunging steps toward them and Sara scrambled to hush her sister, stroking her hair and begging her to quiet down.

Kiara continued to sob, but buried her face in her sister's sweatshirt, which muffled it enough to calm the man. Sara continued the rhythmic strokes down the back of her head, her fingers gently tracing the tight braids, not just to calm her sister but to give her something to focus on to ground her mind.

"You're not going to scream," the man said, taking another two steps closer, now only ten feet from the girls, "Or you'll get hurt. I wouldn't want that. Two pretty little girls like you. It'd be so sad if something happened to you."

Sara's eyes darted back and forth between the tire iron, held nonchalantly in the man's left hand, and his face, white and sticky like spoiled milk. The dark eyes glistened, and though his face stayed soft and limp, revealing no expression, his eyes almost twinkled in their dreadful glee.

"You're not a cop," Sara said, and the man laughed without joy.

"Maybe you're right." His words slipped out smooth as quicksilver and took with them any last semblance of safety or reality.

Sara felt herself float away from her body. She looked down to watch herself from far above. An uncanny feeling of electricity pulsed through her.

"Someone will see you and you'll get in big trouble."

"There's no one. You and I both know it."

Sara's eyes darted to the car, at the gap between it and the wall, measuring and calculating, but the man watched her and knew what she was thinking. She shifted her weight, ready to grab Kiara's arm, ready to run.

"Before you do that," the man's voice startled and stalled her, "think for one second. Maybe you'll get away, but she won't."

Sara held back tears as she realized he was right. She didn't need more than half a second to imagine the dash around the car; her sister stumbling, falling, and being left behind. Kiara would cry as she left her, taking long strides down the ramps to the door, the hall, their apartment. She might make it, but Kiara never would.

"I want to go home," Kiara shrieked into her sweater.

"What do you want from us?" Sara's voice strained to ask through her tears.

"Just get in the car. Both of you. You'll be alright. It'll all be fine if you just do what I say."

The man took a step back toward the open car door, relaxed just enough, and Sara darted to the wall facing the passenger door. Her open palms pressed against the cool concrete, ready to push off and run. His eyes glanced at Kiara then back, the metal tool twitching in his now unsteady hand. Kiara stared at her sister, wide-eyed again and cries softened from shock.

Moments and memories flashed through Sara's mind as her consciousness floated above the scene. She saw the moment her mom walked through the front door, bringing her baby sister home from the hospital: small, dusky, and swaddled in a pink blanket with little birds all over it. Then the time her mother showed her how to feed her new sister with the bottle and even how to rock her to sleep. Next, the fishing trip with their dad last summer and she remembered Kiara accidentally knocking the entire lure box into the lake, her tears, how she'd taken the blame for her sister, and how that night Kiara had crawled into bed with her after their dad had gone to sleep, hugging her tightly and whispering "thank you."

"You'd leave her?" the man asked, a hint of disbelief beneath the cruel steel tone.

"Listen! Just listen, okay?" The words tumbled out fast as Sara watched herself as if from above, sinewy and strong. "I'll run. I can make it back and you know it. You'll get caught."

"You'd abandon your sister?" He sneered. He tried to hide it, but disgust and fear crept across his face.

"If I run, you're done. But if I don't," Sara took a deep breath to steady herself. Her own fear coursed through her veins like boiling water. "But—but—what if I don't? If I get in there, you'll let her go."

"Why?" As he asked, he raised the tire iron and stepped toward the trembling five-year-old. She called out to her big sister in a voice raspy from crying.

"Because if you let her go, you won't get caught. She's just a little kid. She's scared. She won't even be able to remember you. Just let her go home. Just promise you'll leave her, and I'll get in." She swallowed hard again and watched herself in awe of her own bravery.

"How do you know I won't just push her in too? Maybe she needs more punishment than you." His eyes slid back to Kiara, and she shuddered under his gaze.

"I don't know that, but I'm saying, I'll go with you if you leave her. Follow whatever you say. Just leave her. Please. I'll do whatever you want. Just promise."

The man shifted his weight from one foot to the other. His face stayed placid, but his eyes revealed a slight softening, a twinkle of pride.

"Fine."

As he spoke, Sara's body flooded with relief. Her arm reached out toward her stunned sister who was murmuring about wanting to go home. From her viewpoint far above her physical body, she knew she was in charge of everything for just a moment, but it was long enough for what she needed to do.

"I'm going to be okay. Kiara, just go home. Okay? Promise you'll go home. Give Momma a hug from me. I'll be back. Don't worry about me." She forced a smile and hesitated, then added, "I love you."

"No, Sara! Don't go!" The little girl pleaded, but Sara opened the passenger door and slid inside. The man looked to the little girl, moved as if to approach her, but then his dark eyes went as pale as his face, his mouth fell open to gape like a fish, and his arms hung limply from slumped shoulders. Kiara gasped at his transformation, but the man just turned to walk back to the car door, stumbling like a zombie, and got in. Kiara watched as the blue car reversed and turned around, maneuvering in and out of a parking spot to face the right direction, then headed slowly down the ramp.

Kiara collapsed to the floor, sitting with her head thrown back, wailing at the ceiling. The wind changed directions just enough that rain now splattered across her face and body as the pangs of grief and fear flowed out of her. She couldn't stand up. She couldn't do anything but cry.

After a few minutes, the tears trailed off and she had nothing left inside her. Her adrenaline stores were emptied, and she felt hollow and light as she stumbled to her feet like a baby who's just learned to stand. She thought of the man's eyes and how strange they had looked for that moment. A gust of wind blew through the garage, chilling her through her clothes, and somehow it reminded her of Sara's breath on her ear when she whispered secrets. A deep pain in her gut told her she'd already wasted too much time. She walked down the first ramp, then the next, and quickened her pace as she got closer to home.

Just then, through the angled gap between levels, she saw the man again. He was walking quickly, tire iron still in hand, arms swinging in time with his hurried steps.

Her breath tucked itself deep into her lungs as she ducked behind a large red truck. His footsteps echoed through the garage as he headed up her ramp. Flattening herself, she struggled to slide under the truck, pulling in her hand and foot just as his feet appeared in her view from the undercarriage.

He didn't stop and she didn't dare breathe more than in tiny shallow flutters. She tried to follow his movement with her ears, but the rain and wind were too loud. She imagined him walking up each ramp, expecting to see her framed in the opening at the top level, and then his surprise when she wasn't there.

She counted in her head, not trying to measure how long it took him, but just to keep herself from screaming.

There he was, running back down the ramp. His feet pounded against the floor, and as he passed the truck, there was rage in his labored breath.

She waited there, taking tiny sips of air and shaking as she expected him to come back and find her any second. Minutes passed. After almost half an hour, she worked up the courage to creep back out.

She peeked from behind the truck, and when she saw he was not there waiting for her, she took a deep breath and sprinted down the final ramp, bursting through the door into the hallway of apartments on the third floor, and leaping past the seven doors before she made it to her own.

Throwing open the door and slamming it behind her, her shaking hands pulled each lock closed, and she found a deeper layer of tears, beginning to cry again. Sobs gushed out of her, arms outstretched in front of her, mouth pulled wide with her two baby teeth missing, as she ran straight into her mother's arms.

"Honey, what's wrong? Hold on," her mother said, pulling her daughter into her lap and then turning her attention briefly to the conference call on her computer. "Sorry guys, I've gotta go. You should have enough to get going. I'll send you the rest of the details later."

Ending the call, she gave her full attention to her daughter, and the gravity of the situation settled in the air around them.

"Baby, tell me what's wrong. Where's Sara? Did I hear the door?"

The story babbled out of Kiara all at once, like turning on a faucet. How they'd snuck out to play, the toy car crash, the light blue car and the sickly white man, the rain, the fear, and how Sara left with him to save her. By the time she had finished that part, she was crying so hard she couldn't bring herself to relive the further fear when she saw him again.

Her mother listened carefully, staying calm despite the tears collecting in the rims of her eyes, and had Kiara repeat the details about the man and his car again as she dialed 911. Halfway through her description of the emergency to the operator, she couldn't hold it in anymore and burst into sobs of her own, making it difficult to understand her and causing the woman on the line to ask her to repeat herself again and again.

"He took my daughter! Dammit, don't you understand? He took her! She's in danger! You need to get here right away!" The mother's words were full of pain, and she pulled Kiara deeper onto her lap, close to her chest.

The girl clutched at her mother's shirt with one hand while she sucked the thumb of the other, something she hadn't done in years. She had thought she'd feel safe with her mom, but the anxiety and emptiness persisted. Her eyes looked through the office doorway, through the living room, back to the locked front door. She couldn't tear them away.

She tried to think of Sara, but something kept every

memory of her sister pushed down, not letting her access even a glimpse of her face. She sighed and cuddled deeper into her mother's arms.

Her eyes stayed glued to the door as her mother's words morphed into indecipherable screams of absolute grief. There was a siren outside the building, but it sounded like it was just passing by. Her entire world shrank to the size of the front door. She imagined the handle turning and felt she couldn't look away, couldn't even blink, or it'd be true.

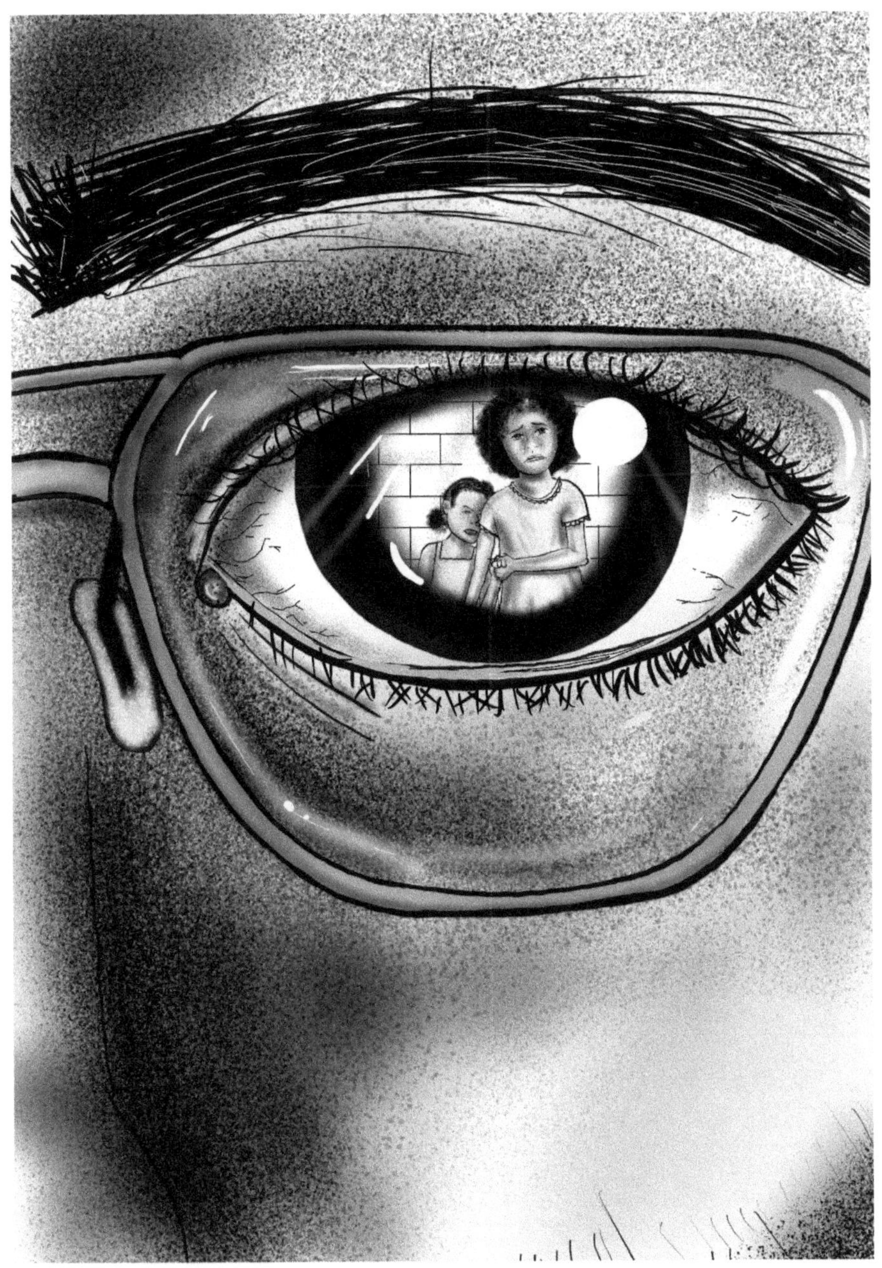

THE PROFOUND PAIN OF LETTING GO

In his kindergarten classroom, Hunter's tongue peeks out from the corner of his mouth as he concentrates on gluing the green leaves of construction paper along the stem of the thumbprint flower. Each painted petal glistens cherry red, his favorite color and one he associates with hearts and roses, things that make his mommy smile and the craft is a Mother's Day present after all. Violet elbows him and he turns to see two crayons hanging from her top lip like tusks or vampire fangs, her hands raised in monster claws.

"Boo!" Violet says, and one of the crayons falls loose. Hunter and the other kids at the "star table," designated by the laminated green star hanging above them, all break into giggles that scatter into the air around them like dropped marbles. Even Ms. Black chuckles as she gently tells them to settle down and finish their projects before circle time.

The last leaf sticks to the glob of glue as Hunter presses down, white stickiness escaping around the edges and the center growing darkly damp. He frowns.

"It's okay, it'll disappear when it dries. Trust me," Ms. Black's voice is velvet soft as she pats his shoulder, and he does trust her. "Your mommy will love it."

She walks aways while Hunter prints his name as neatly as he can across the top of the page. The second his fingers form the final "r," wobbling and hooked backward, Violet's hand darts to the edge of the page and scribbles a wavy black line of crayon.

"Hey!" Hunter shouts, his face dark and aghast while Violet grins, her tongue toeing out between a missing front tooth. "You ruined it."

"Oh no, Violet," Ms. Black says, briskly walking back toward the table. That's when the sound down the hallway startles everyone to silence. Hunter wonders why there would be fireworks inside the school. Wouldn't that be dangerous? He knows to keep away from them, the way his father warned him again and again to stay back while he lit showers of colorful fire and Hunter held the sparkler last summer at the picnic. But no, this isn't fireworks. It's too loud, snapping and unsettling his stomach like the surprise clatter of pots and pan falling when you open a kitchen cabinet.

Ms. Black is shouting, pointing at the corner of the room, running toward the door to press against it, her face a crumpled web of lines as she strains, but the door flies open anyway. Everyone is screaming, crying, shrieking. The entire world filled with unbearable noise. Some duck down, hide under desks.

Others follow their teacher's orders, running to the corner like they'd practiced and cowering together in a warm, whimpering pile. Hunter can't move. His feet have become cinderblocks, cemented to the floor.

Fluorescent light frames the man in the door, pouring around him like a halo eclipsed by the dark camouflage of his outfit. Hunter stares at the man's face, the lower half obscured by a black cloth, but his eyes shine hard as diamonds, full of a hatred that slides down the child's spine with a shivering, unthawable frost.

The room erupts in gunfire and Hunter screams. Violet grabs his arm, her palm wet and sticky. She says something he can't understand, only the shrill terror in her voice as it gnaws through the explosions. He covers his ears, shuts his eyes as tightly as possible, flashes of light still forcing their way past his eyelids. Then it all stops.

Slowly, Hunter unshutters his vision. The man is gone. Ms. Black is gone. The other children have disappeared. There is no one left in the room except Hunter. The classroom is dark, the overhead lights, hallways lights, even the red salt lamp in the reading corner have all extinguished. Through the closed blinds, a weak, gray light from an overcast sky filters through, painting sickly stripes across the floor. The stench of sulfur and sweat that had wafted strongly through the air a moment prior has completely dissipated, and the air smells faintly electric, like burnt cables or old library carpet.

"Hello?" he calls out, his voice bouncing back to him from the wall of artwork fluttering under the vent, the illustrated alphabet banner over the blank whiteboard, the five round tables each surrounded by small blue chairs. The word falls away in the heaviness of the air, the breath in his lungs trembling and the urge to weep filling his body, but his eyes and voice refuse to cooperate. With small tentative steps, he walks around the classroom, bending over and checking under tables and in cubbies, as if his classmates were just hiding from him.

The only sound in the room is the low, familiar yet nebulous hum, far in the background, sizzling in a light static buzz. A queasy fear pulses through him as he searches, but it begins to wane after his third lap around the classroom, replaced with a heavy emptiness that sits on his heart like a weight. Sitting in Ms. Black's chair at the front of the room, his legs pulled to his chest as he sinks into the cushion, Hunter's gaze falls on the open door.

The hallway outside is darker than the classroom, with no windows to pour even the sickly gray light of day into the void that waits. He doesn't want to go into the hall, but voicelessly, it calls to him. Fingers clenched around the doorframe, he peers out, expecting a light, but the hallway instead morphs into a darkening void the farther it goes from the slight illumination of the classroom. Filled with unspeakable dread, he pulls himself back into the room, pressing the heavy door closed. The latch clicks and a long, thin shudder pulls itself from his lungs.

Crawling into Ms. Black's chair again, he rubs at his eyes, holds himself tightly and rocks, sniffling and shivering, but eventually the tears wane. Several books are stacked on the easel next to the chair. Hunter pulls each one into his lap, his finger moving under the words, sounding out those he can, his eyes tracing over the watercolor illustrations of happy children, anthropomorphic animals, and fantastical scenery. His heart slows and his head gets heavy, and he imagines it filling with sand like the hourglass his art teacher uses for free draw time. Setting the last book back on the easel, he scoots to the edge of the chair, his feet dangling before reaching the floor.

Pulling his backpack from his cubby, he unzips it and digs through the crumpled papers, spare clothes, and plastic baggie of crackers he'd brought for snack before his small hand finds what he's searching for, the hard plastic edge of the rocket ship grasped between his fingers. He'd brought it even though toys from home were against the rules, and laughs at his tiny rebellion as the mess spills onto the floor, pulled from the backpack's depths. Standing up, he sputters and whooshes the way he imagines a real rocket would as he spins; the spacecraft under the guidance of his gentle hand. However, after a few moments of joy, the feeling fades and, puzzled, he realizes he can't remember how to play anymore. With a sigh, he sets the rocket down, but there's no sorrow in the abandoned game.

Hunter scans the murky gray room again, his eyes settling on the corner near the window with its drawn blinds. Far off in his mind, somewhere unreachable, a memory of his classmates piled there, faces blanched and wide terrified eyes, flashes in his mind. The air feels thick, as if he's swimming through it, when he moves to the corner. There's a warmth there waiting for him, and without knowing why, he closes his eyes and bends over with pursed lips, pretending to kiss each of his friends' foreheads he'd seen in his distant memory. With every kiss, some of the heaviness lifts, and when he finishes, the stagnant warm air evaporates, leaving the corner as cold and sterile as the rest of the room. A pang of loneliness ripples through him, yet a calm clarity follows, and the corners of the five-year-old's lips twitch into a small smile.

He thinks of Ms. Black and the image of her face, scared, heartbroken, and weary, appears to him at the front of the room. Hunter crawls back into her familiar chair, his cheek nuzzling the soft backing as he pretends to cuddle into his beloved teacher.

"It's okay, Ms. Black. You were always the best teacher ever," he whispers into the cushion, and he thinks he hears a soft sigh before a warmth deep in the chair rises through him. Once again, the room is numbly cool.

As Hunter walks back to his seat at the star table, he imagines himself floating. His body feels light and airy, a tingle of fear nesting in the back of his mind that he'll blow away into nothingness any second. Sitting in the blue plastic chair, it's warm, as if he'd only just left it a moment ago and not the stretch of time that unfurled in slow-motion in the dark classroom. He turns to where Violet sat, the two crayon fangs lying where they'd fallen.

"Violet?" Hunter's voice is a dry scratch through his tight throat.

Reaching out, he hugs the air, pretending she's inside his empty embrace. When he pulls away, a shimmer cracks through the darkness and he thinks he sees her face, but it's not the silly, sometimes annoying girl who makes him giggle and steals his markers. It's her face, but soaked with tears, dripping wet to match her hands, which drip with something bright red like the paint for his thumbprint flowers, but he swallows hard, knowing it's something different that he won't let his brain register.

A distorted whimpering voice pierces through him, somehow Violet's and yet not. Pure sincerity rings through a thick desolate insulation of fear, and she says, "I'm sorry I ruined your drawing."

He wants to cry, but there are no tears left, his body dry like an autumn leaf, lighter with each moment, the edges of his consciousness growing fuzzy and threatening to flow away into the ether.

"It's okay."

"But it was for your momma." The voice has become a faint wail, like wind through an old house.

"It doesn't matter. Mommy will love it anyway."

The howling of her voice quiets into the one he'd grown to love over the school year.

"You're a good friend, Hunter. Thank you."

"I'm going to miss you," he says, reaching out where the shimmer had been, but it doesn't return, only fingertips through air.

"Don't be scared. You're the bravest kid in the class." Violet's voice has softened to a whisper he has to strain to hear. "Remember when you caught that spider on Ms. Black's desk and let it go in the grass?" Her laughter is a twinkle of light behind his eyes, pulling his mouth into a reluctant smile.

"Yeah."

"Just be brave like that. You'll be okay."

"But I don't want to be brave," he says, his voice a tiny mewl, but she's gone. He's alone in the drafty classroom of shadows again.

Elbows on the table, he presses his eyes into his palms then slowly claws his fingers through his hair, an electric tingle as his fingernails scrape across his scalp. His head lolls down and his gaze finds the craft for his mommy. His lips quiver as he wishes he could say goodbye to her before he has to leave, but as he loses himself in the red flowers, green paper leaves, and black scribble from Violet, he breathes out long and slow.

The whisper from the vent above rustles the paper leaves as he sets the craft down; it doesn't mean anything anymore. Once it was important, but now he can't remember why. He can't remember anything before this room.

His body has grown heavy again since he sat down; it's a difficult journey across the room back to the door. Like a sand-filled glove, he rests his hand on the handle and nudges the door open again. The hallway is still cold and empty, but it doesn't terrify him any longer. He wants to be alone. As he staggers into the darkness, he thinks of how desperately tired his small body is, and how nice it'll be to rest at last. With each step into the absolute darkness, the weight falls away, first from his limbs, then his torso, and finally his head floats like a petal on the breeze. In the last moment before he lets go, he wishes he could've had a little more time. He hears the door close far behind him, and he surrenders himself to the darkness.

DYIN' AIN'T NOTHIN' BUT FALLIN' ASLEEP

I don't know why everyone's so scared of dyin'. It's not that big of a deal. Sure, you're gone for a few minutes or so, but then bam, they just zap you back. I've seen Dad do it a billion times, back when he drove the ambulance. There's nothin' to it at all. It's just the same as fallin' asleep, then you wake up all groggy, don't know where you're at for a minute, but you're fine. Back to boring normal. Just wake up like it's nothin'.

Yeah, it's true that sometimes they need oxygen and shit like bags of blood when they're bleedin' all over the goddamn place. Tide them over until the doctors fix 'em up, right as rain. The only people who die permanent-like are old people, and that's 'cause Dad's zapper can't restart their old, worn-out, leathery hearts. When stuff gets too old, it just breaks beyond repair, ya know? I ain't scared of it, no matter what Tony says, not when

I've seen people snap back like I have with my own eyes.

That's what I'm thinkin' about when I walk the "guilt processional," smilin' a smug-ass smirk when I find Kev and Tony in the google-eyed crowd. They're all snotty, like they really think they're never gonna see me again. Bunch of babies. I told them the stories about Dad enough times, you'd think they'd calm down.

Before he got laid off, Dad used to take me all over, hidden in his ambulance so I didn't have to go to school. Not that they really cared anymore, so I probably didn't actually have to hide, but it made it more fun. Like a secret between just me and Dad. I loved it. Sure, Dad would yell when he caught me messin' with the supplies, and I had to shut up when he was talkin' to a patient, but mostly we were happy. Those were the good times, before the stupid "Uprising" bullshit ruined everything.

I wouldn't be up here if it wasn't for those assholes. Every little mistake equals a death sentence now, and in front of everyone to boot. Like they've gotta make it embarrassing, as if dyin' wasn't enough of a punishment. My face is burnin' bright red already, I can tell by the tingle like a slap on my cheeks, but I breathe in deep and slow, tryin' to shake it off before anyone notices.

As I'm walkin' by the crowd, I remember sometimes people peed or even shit their pants when they died. I hope I don't do that. I couldn't stand to have everyone calling me "piss pants" forever. I'd rather stay dead.

The man in front of me is draggin' his feet, nearly trippin' me with the goddamn rope securing our legs together in this ridiculous shame parade. I wish he'd just suck it up. It's not that bad. Let's get it over and done with already.

The crowd is bigger than I'd thought, and I spit between two airheads staring at me with vapid blue eyes. Of course, everybody's gotta come out to this fuckin' abandoned mall to gawk at the "criminals." Yeah, yeah, stealing is wrong, whatever, but it was just a cheapo squirt gun. A *squirt gun* for god's sake. I can't help it that they'd jacked up the price so much that Dad couldn't afford it for my birthday. He was so sad, his eyes got all wet like he was gonna cry. Made my stomach squirm like I swallowed a fistful of worms. So I slipped it under my shirt, no big deal.

That guy at the register could've been cool, not called me out like that, but no, now I'm here, getting fucking executed over a toy. Fuck, it couldn't have been somethin' a little more badass? It's extra mortifying getting killed over a toy at twelve years old. I should've swiped somethin' else. *Anything* else. Even a candy bar or pack of gum would've been better to die over than a squirt gun, like I'm still a goddamn toddler. Oh well, the boys had their laugh about it, but look who's got goddamn tears runnin' down their faces like babies and who's the one keepin' his cool.

The girl behind me is cryin' real hard. I keep hearing her snorkin' back globs of snot, choking on it sometimes, then gaspin' before letting another big ol' shriek out. I wish she'd shut up. It's killin' my ears. I look over my shoulder to hush her, to explain that it's just a temporary thing, no need to be actin' up like that, if she'll listen over her own screamin', but my voice catches in my throat and disappears.

She's a real baby. Gotta be only seven or eight. Maybe less. What could she have possibly done? Stolen a squirt gun too? The thought turns the bile in my stomach, lurchin' it up, but I keep it down. Turning around fast, before I let the overwhelmin' urge to bawl creep up my throat. Never let it reach my face. Stay hard. Chew it up, push it down, swallow, clench my fists. Gotta be strong, buddy. You've got this.

In the torn-up remnants of what used to be a food court, on the stage where they used to have kid beauty pageants and choir concerts, ten chairs wait for us. One of the overhead fluorescent lights flickers a little like we're in some low budget horror flick, and others are missin', just wires danglin' down like untied nooses. I notice a dingy Panda Express sign is still hangin' by one edge in the corner. What a joke. A laugh comes out as a dry cough. I look back at the boys, their eyes still wide and glistenin' wet.

Where's Dad? I can't stop myself, my eyes search the crowd, scannin' every face, but I don't see him.

A twinge of fear prickles the hair across the back of my neck. Who's gonna bring me back if Dad doesn't show? I look around, but I don't see any paramedics, at least not in uniform. Thinkin' back, I haven't seen one filin' into these shows in ages. So, who brings 'em back? A shudder tickles down my spine, but I hide it as best I can.

No, he'll show. Dad always comes through. He'll come save me.

The soldiers file out, faces obscured by those stupid masks so nobody can recognize them, or spit in their face. Pretty much nobody complains about the executions anymore, not like when they first started. Guess Dad's right that people can get used to anything.

I wonder if it's gonna hurt. Another flicker of fear runs through me. I can be a bit of a wimp about pain, even if I like to pretend I'm not. When Kev dared me to jump that ditch and I broke my arm, I had to rub my face in the mud to hide the tears. And the bone wasn't even stickin' out or anything. I know dyin' can hurt real bad sometimes.

As the soldiers set up, we're prodded along, the rope attachin' us just long enough for everyone to sit in their designated wooden chair. Sweat beads at my temples and my shirt is sticking to my back. I wipe at my face. It's not even hot in here.

I glance to the right. The stumblin' man finally manages to make it to his seat, then immediately slumps forward. His face is too relaxed, lips droopin' open like a dog. He's gotta be drunk. I slide away from him, to the edge of my seat, near the still screamin' little girl.

The eyes of the crowd are vicious. Everybody's always out for blood nowadays. Nothin' ever satisfies 'em neither. Only a few here and there are wet and weepy for us. Probably not even sad, probably just pity. Or maybe they're cryin' for themselves, seeing themselves up here for some stupid crime and thanking the heavens that they didn't get caught like us dumbos.

I do notice a bit of softness when their eyes turn toward the girl though. The little thing's still sobbin' and carrying on. Bastards. Like I'm not a kid, too? Naw, just a punk to these jerks. Well, joke's on them because I know Dad's gonna be here soon, and he's gonna save me.

After we saw that first execution, when we were walking back home, I told Dad I'd never let them kill him. He'd smiled, said he appreciated that, and that if they ever tried to get me, he'd be up on that stage punching them out in a heartbeat. That made me smile real big. I know the only reason he could be late is because it's part of some plan to bust me out of here. There's no doubt in my mind he'll save me and we'll get out of this stinkin' dump of a city. Sneak somewhere and hide. Go to some small backwoods place they haven't taken over yet. Then we can break whatever rules we want without anyone breathin' down our neck. Mom should come too, but she's always so afraid of breakin' the rules, it might be best to just leave her behind. She'd never get in trouble like me and Dad.

I rub my sweaty palms down the front of my jeans. You know, I'd never even heard of a garrote before the Uprising. Dad says they brought back medieval shit as scare tactics. I'll admit, that first public execution was scary. They don't even have the decency to cover anyone's fuckin' eyes. No, they want you to look into the fear and pain, and for the poor bastards up there to look out and plead for you to follow their stupid rules, behave like good little kids.

I swallow hard. I guess I'm the poor bastard now.

Where the hell is Dad?

Back then, the mall still looked like a mall. It was ridiculous, like some dumb old TV show, with old fast-food smells and the remains of Halloween decorations still hangin' on the wall nearby. Little handprint bats made by preschoolers. I flinch as the image focuses in my mind. No, don't let them get to you. It's all just theatrics. Gotta please the crowd, that's why it's gotta be worse and worse, more and more often. No, don't worry. Dad'll save me.

I scan the crowd, but I can't find Kev or Tony anymore. How could they leave their best friend's execution? I imagine them outside hurlin' their guts out. That's probably all. They just cried so much they had to go barf. When I told them about the zapper, they just kept tellin' me I was wrong, like they were experts. As if my own dad, a trained EMS worker, couldn't revive me even though I've seen him do it about a million times. The color just drained outta their faces, and they kept shakin' their heads, voices low and droning on about "it's not like that" and "come on, you know better." They can be such morons sometimes.

The soldiers have started at the first chair. I can tell by the way the crowd goes completely silent, all eyes on the sputtering, squeaking throat of the woman at the far end. I don't want to look. Makes my stomach flip just thinking of the way they look when it's done. Bulgin' eyes, red and purple face, hands pullin' at the tightenin' rope. Nope. I can't stand to look at it. Not since that first one. Mom said I didn't need to see that kind of stuff, and though I tried to act all hard and argue, I agreed. For once, Mom was right about something, so Dad didn't take me to any more executions, and I always found an excuse to get out of it when the boys suggested we sneak in and watch. They never seemed to mind. I don't know why anybody would wanna see something like that to be honest.

It all goes much faster than I remember. How long have we been up here? The quickest glance tells me they're already on the third one. Scanning the crowd again and again, I don't see them. Where's Dad? Where's Mom?

No, I don't want Mom to see me like this. I begged Dad not to tell her. Still, as I bite the inside of my cheek and tap my foot nervously, I kinda wish she was here. Yeah, maybe it's babyish, but I want my mom right now. She always makes everything better. Even her smell is nice. Kind of like fresh-baked bread.

Right then, as my eyes are getting too full and salty to hold the tears back anymore, I see them. Mom's draggin' Dad behind her, pushing them to the front. She's sheet white and screamin' stuff like "stop" and "that's my boy," so of course the crowd starts mumblin' and talking right away, drowning her out. God, I've never been so happy to see someone in my whole life.

"It's okay, Mom. Dad's got a plan. He'll get me out of here," I shout to her, but the way she stares, lip quiverin' and eyes all wobbly and confused, I don't think she heard me. I try again, louder. "Dad! Did you bring the zapper, just in case?"

He's just looking at my feet, his mouth scrunched up all funny. Can't they hear me? Mom's screaming again, not even making words, just screechin' and fallin' on her knees, her dark hair coming loose to stick all over her face. Normally, I'd be embarrassed, especially with the way everyone is lookin' at her, but instead that prickle of fear is electric all over my body again, making every hair stand on end. And Dad's hunched over, inchin' away from her like he doesn't know her. I see him rubbin' at his eyes, face gone red and sweaty. He's lookin' at her as he backs away, just rubbin' his eyes again and again. Tears slip past his hands, makin' trails down his dirty cheeks. Why won't he look at me?

"Dad!" I shout, but he's ignorin' me. I don't understand. He knows I'm up here. He's gotta hear me, recognize my voice. Mom pulled him all the way here, why won't he look?

Some soldiers are pushing through the crowd, pullin' Mom to her feet, draggin' her toward the exit. I'm cryin' now. I don't even care about holdin' it together anymore. I want my mom.

Then my breath freezes solid in my lungs. I can't believe what I'm seeing. Dad turns around, real slow-like, his head droopin' down. He's following her out.

"Dad! Wait!"

But he doesn't stop. He's shufflin' like an old man out through the parted crowd. I start to hyperventilate. The drunk guy right next to me is having the rope slipped over his head, the wooden stick twisted and tightened.

Why is he leavin' without me? What happened to the plan? Why didn't he bring the paddles? I'm breathin' so fast, I feel I could pass out any second.

They're done with the drunk man. I look at him, his body totally limp, head bent back, the red ligature marks deep and ragged like burns.

"No! I don't wanna die! I didn't do nothin' wrong! It was just a mistake!"

I don't even realize it's me shoutin' at first. The girl next to me is cryin' again. She gets up, tries to run away, but the rope at her feet trips her to the ground. Soldiers are helping her back into her chair, petting her hair like an animal as someone slips the rope over my head.

It's happening. Maybe the boys were right. I jam my hands up, but it's too late. My fingers pry at the rope, but I can't get under it. My head is heavy and full, throbbin'. It hurts! I can't breathe! I want to grab at the soldier, try to stop him, but my hands won't obey. They clutch and claw at the rope as it draws tighter and tighter.

I'd thought I wanted it to be fast, get it over with, but not anymore. Give me one more second. Just one more. Please, just let me breathe. Let me crawl into my mommy's lap and fall asleep there, not here. Not here, in front of everyone, yet all alone.

Then something inside me cracks and shatters, and I'm left exposed. Dumb. Broken. I realize I've been wrong. Maybe I'm not comin' back. Even if Dad was here with the zapper.

Conversations with Dad in the ambulance rush back to me in a sickening blur. Sometimes they wouldn't make it. Sometimes the paddles didn't work, and they couldn't come back, but Dad tried to hide it. He'd said the hospital could fix them, modern medicine and all, as he'd cover the face with a sheet so I didn't have to look at it. Didn't have to accept it. I didn't wanna believe it could just be over like that, no matter how young or healthy you'd been a moment before. I'd always let myself believe they could bring them back.

Shame eclipses fear for just a moment. An intense urge to suck my thumb, somethin' I haven't done for a decade, washes over me, but my hands won't listen. They just pry at the rope until the nails chip off, slippery, warm, and desperate.

My eyes bulge as I struggle, fuzzy clouds of darkness closing in from all sides. Why didn't you save me, Dad? You're supposed to be here, to stop the bad guys so we can get away.

I want my mommy. Please, come back, Mommy. I should've listened to you.

My ears are filled with my muffled heartbeat behind cotton. The light is just a pinprick and I'm ready to go. The fear is leavin'. I swear I feel Mommy's hand on my face, hear her voice, and behind it, electric whirrin' as the charge builds. The world goes black.

PORTAGE, OHIO IN EARLY AUTUMN

A dozen people tread through the corn. Insects fall and writhe against their careful hands as they part the stalks, cursing under their breath for not sowing the seeds in tidy, even rows. Instead, the plants grew nestled close together, their rows zigzagging mazelike across the miles of flat land.

She is missing. Callie. Five years old. Blonde. Apple cheeks. Last seen in a blue nightgown with a tiny pink rose sewn on the collar. She isn't from here. She's a stranger, but they band together to find the child. It's a cold morning and she didn't take her shoes. Illness, hypothermia, and bad press for the small town all hum in the farmers' minds. There's an unspoken urgency.

Her grandmother tells through tears and yellow teeth, "I woke up and she was gone."

Her sheets still smell of sleep and the front door, unlocked, is still ajar.

There's no need for police. She's certainly wandered into the corn. Being from the city, she didn't know the instant disorientation when you step in and the world closes behind you. She must be crying, cowering against the hard earth, or still searching for a way out. They imagine her breath in the cold air, timid puffs like smoke.

Confident they'll find her, they think of bringing her back to her grandmother's sturdy arms, roped with blue veins from hard labor, her open calloused hands, speckled with age spots and broken capillaries.

The girl's name rings across the fields, muffled through the guest room window where she'd slept and dreamt of riding horses along the gravel road.

"Come out, Callie! Shout and we'll find you!"

Mottled purple, under the bed, she cannot hear them calling for her. Nightgown stuffed down her throat, eyes open, staring blindly toward the bedroom door where his shadow had appeared, finger to lips, whispering in a gruff yet trembling voice, "Stay quiet."

She'd laughed when her grandmother told her about ears of corn and potato eyes. She'd dashed into the backyard and shrieked with joy while chasing the black and white chickens. When her grandmother milked Ol' Bessie, she'd helped tug the udder and tasted the sweet, warm milk. She'd licked her lips. It was nothing like the cold, processed stuff from the grocery store.

Now, she doesn't hear them calling. She can't hear their voices, the buzz of the two flies already circling her ripening body, nor the crying of her grandmother in the living room. Only the corn listens with its deaf ears. No longer can her lips form the words to tell them that the voice she'd heard last night still trembles as he shouts her name.

His eyes dart back to her window when no one is watching. He can't help himself. A voice carries on the wind, faint and light, but he can't make out the words. He doesn't recognize it, but he winces when he remembers that he never let her speak.

He walks farther, calling her name while his boots stick in the mud. Behind him, he can feel her watching through the walls from her hiding spot with open, glassy eyes.

THE NIGHT VISITOR

Now that you have begun reading this, the Night Visitor will come to you. There is no use panicking and closing the book, pretending you never opened it to begin with. There is no going back. No running from your fate. No stopping his steady travel toward you, even now, rousing from sleep and working his way through time and space to you. Instead, you should take a deep breath and embrace the inevitable visit. The Night Visitor has been called to you by your deepest longing. That's what brought you to this book, drove you to open it to this page to find this message, just for you.

You are to be his host, but don't worry, he will not stay long.

When he comes, the Night Visitor will not care if you're sleeping, telling yourself this was all a hoax or nightmare, or if you're awake, waiting for him, or cowering under blankets. Your door may be locked or left open; it matters not. The Night Visitor does not travel like you or me. He will be there, by your bed, announced by the soft rustle of dead leaves and quiet flap of skin-stretched wings. Before you see him, the room will become a sudden vacuum, devoid of air, leaving you gasping. He enjoys the bulging eyes and fish wheezes of his hosts, but understands your mortality, so soon a wind races back into the room and you can breathe once more.

If you have chosen to hide like a child, he will approach your bed slowly, marinating you in anticipation. Cloth pulls across your skin as he uncovers you, two wide eyes staring down at you in the darkness, glistening sclera shining all 'round beads of black. Your muscles ripple as a shudder shoots down your spine.

His form is incomprehensible, an amalgamation of bones and scraps of skin connected perversely, some tied invisibility together so they appear to float in the void of your dark room. No hands nor feet appear at the ends of his limbs, but strange appendages, otherworldly, sharp, and terrible. Something grows from his neck, branching like a brittle collar of alien coral around his dark face, no expression or features visible beyond the night-marish orbs suspended in the abyss, fixed on you.

You will invariably open your mouth to scream, but not even a hoarse, forced squeak will squeeze free. The Night Visitor steps forward, one long arm hovering over you as you lean back on the bed, trying to sink into your mattress to avoid his touch. Your legs are concrete, anchoring you, and yet you want nothing but to flee. The arm lowers slowly, the tall form bending, bringing the moon-yellow ringed eyes closer and closer. When the tip of the bone appendage touches you, it's as sharp as a scalpel, tearing through skin as easily as damp tissue, but you do not flinch. The Night Visitor will get to work right away.

Wringing your flesh between kneading knobs of bone, you'll be surprised to feel no pain. Your human form cracks, dissolves in on itself, meshing into a malleable living clay the Night Visitor rolls into a long snake then coils around himself. As you weave between jutting bones and through skin that feels serpentine against your trembling new construct, there is no terror. Only sublime bliss to be incorporated into the Night Visitor for however long he'll keep you. Because you expressed fear, he soothes you, turns you into the submissive pet you've always longed to become. You will not need to fend for yourself; being a part of his form, he makes all decisions, takes care of all needs, and you merely must exist.

But say you don't curl in on yourself, trembling under sheets and quilts, when the Night Visitor approaches. Perhaps you plan to stay awake into the dreamlike witching hour when he makes his appearance. Your chosen fate will be quite different.

Impressed by your bravery, or delusional insistence against his existence, the Night Visitor will enter your room with the lumbering gait and hunched figure of an old man. In the dim lamp light, you see his face full of boils and growths, bubbling over his brow to conceal his eyes. His mouth twists up in an agonized grin and in each gnarled hand he carries a gift for the victim bold enough to accept their destiny and face him.

In the left, a large copper coin, green patina growing over the unfamiliar face embossed on its side. In the right, a small ornate wooden box with a gold latch. As he gets closer, he lifts both arms, presenting the gifts on upturned palms. He won't have to say a word for you to understand that you must choose. A reward presented to the hero who faces the monster despite the tension in every muscle, so tight you feel you may snap like a rubber band at any moment. A silent whisper tingles the base of your brain: *brave or curious?*

You reach out for the coin, and he relinquishes it. Turning the coin in your hand, a nauseating cloud of dust appears, choking you. As you cough, you realize the Night Visitor is gone. You have made your choice, and the coin proves a good luck charm as the weeks fly by, each more prosperous than the last. Money seems to fall into your hands, whether through fortunate business dealings, unexpected generous gifts, or lucky ventures. You return a lost wallet and get rewarded, money mysteriously appears in your bank account, you buy a scratch-off and win a hundred thousand dollars. And yet, despite the wealth you're quickly amassing, other parts of your life begin to decay. Friendships fall away, relatives pick fights out of envy, side-eye you and quit inviting you to gatherings, and coworkers whisper about you just out of earshot, the venom of their eyes stinging when they catch your own.

You try to dispose of the coin, but no matter where you throw it or who you pawn it off on, it finds its way back to your bedside table. You reread this book, trying to call the Night Visitor back to your side, to make another choice, but he never returns. You hide away with your riches, becoming a lonely miser but never wanting for material things.

Or you instead reach out for the small box, wanting to avoid this selfish fate. Maybe you can't stand the mystery of what secrets it holds. Even if it's empty, you need to know. He sets it firmly in your grasp, a sick smile painted on his misshapen lips. As you open it, the Night Visitor creeps soundlessly out through the bedroom door.

Inside the box, there is a tiny scroll of parchment. Carefully, you'll remove it, unrolling it to reveal inked scratches in an alphabet you've never seen before. Your mind ignites with insatiable intrigue. You must decipher it, discover what secrets it holds, and become enlightened to the knowledge of the Night Visitor.

Years fly by, filled with days and nights among the stacks. The rest of your dreams and aspirations fall away to this obsession. Soon, you find yourself proficient in dozens of languages and a scholar in multitudes of ancient texts. You scour dusty tomes in libraries around the world, and every cent is spent on travel to exotic lands; however, you struggle to enjoy your travels. There can be no rest, no enjoyment until the scroll is decoded.

Your spine curves, permanently hunched from reading worn books at tables drenched in candlelight. Your hair grows matted, an unkempt mane of wild frizz, and then thins, leaving neglected patches of scalp visible past the wiry gray hair. Growths appear across your face and body, some so large they hinder your fingers as they struggle to turn page after page, others partially blinding you as they droop heavily from your brow. Still, you continue your quest.

It is not until one late night in your old age, alone in a foreign country, at a forgotten corner of the local university's library, that your eyes light up, enlightenment washing across your weary face.

You read the scroll, understanding every word. Euphoria erupts from the depths of your gut, spurring your heart to race. As you finish the final word of the scroll, a sharp pain cracks down your left arm and your vision dims. You relax, a crooked smile on your lips as you collapse against the wood grain of the desk, savoring the metallic taste of the unspoken words on your tongue.

You've read this far and have decided none of the prior destinies feel right to wear as your own. Instead, you long for another option, and there is one more. It is not to flee, for the Night Visitor will visit wherever you find yourself at that late hour this coming night. There is no location he will not visit. Instead, your challenge is to sleep. Slumber soundly even knowing that he will be at your bedside soon. This is the choice of the dreamer. *Are you a dreamer?*

You stir slightly when he sits at the foot of your bed, his weight compressing the mattress just enough for you to register his presence, but still, you do not fully wake. He leans closer, pressing his body against yours, his ragged breathing heavy against your ear, his skeletal fingers playing with your hair. You do not wake, do not allow yourself to wake, and so he joins you not only in your bed, but your dreamscape.

In your mind, you are transported to a dark room. A skeletal being, the orifices of his skull fused closed to render him faceless and dripping molten gold from his aureate bones, you recognize him as your Night Visitor, even without having seen him before. He moves toward you and you find yourself drawn to him; globules of metal sear down your skin as you embrace, but the pain is ecstatic.

He moves rhythmically against you, the lipless mouth pressed to yours, his teeth burning through your fleshy face, marrying the bones beneath with his own. When he flips you over and takes you, ramming into your most tender tissue so you smell the burning meat and hear the sizzle of destroyed skin, your corporeal form unites with him in the real world, pressing backward with eager pleasure against your lover.

The Night Visitor moves gently in the real world, but in your dream, he rends you to pieces, tearing deeper with each thrust. You squirm against him, mind and body, the otherworldly pleasure transcendent, leaving you breathless.

When his face peels open, blooming like a rare flower, the petals reaching out to you, caressing your face with slick gore, you smile in your sleep. His body unravels, strips of pale skin, amber fat, and crimson muscle, wrapping around you, coiling tightly around your limbs in an embrace unlike any you will ever feel again. When you give yourself to him fully, he reciprocates.

If you choose to love the Night Visitor, you will still be sleeping when he leaves. When the sunlight creeps through your blinds, ending the dream quiver of your eyelids, you will find your body sore, violated, and strangely empty. A rainbow of bodily fluids smeared across every inch of skin, but despite your panic, you find yourself intact and unharmed.

You shower, scrub away the stains, but he has left his mark on you. You will never experience anything so terrible yet wonderful again, but you will spend your life searching, finding a spectrum of experiences along your journey. This is his gift for you.

If you've read this far, not snapping the book shut and swearing this is all a hoax, some kind of cruel gimmick, then you must know this is the truth. The Night Visitor will come, and no matter your choice, while each may seem horrific, they are gifts. He is coming tonight. Be a good host, welcome him, and send my regards.

Even after all these decades, how I miss him so.

THROUGH THE HOLLER, INTO THE DARK

The raw white of the trimmed fat threatens to dribble through my fingers as I carry it across the yard. Blood trickles down my arm, dripping from my elbow into the bare dirt, leaving a tiny trail behind me until I reach the high grass. Daddy would be mad to know I'm wasting it, say it'd be good for greasing a pan, but he wouldn't understand. Nobody would except maybe Bonnie.

Counting the steps, twenty-three forward, sixteen to the left, the slippery meat warms in my hand, matching my own temperature. I almost step on the skull, nearly falling backward to avoid my bare foot crunching down on the ancient thing, but a surge of relief flutters through me. It's still there. Right where I remembered it.

The fanged skull stares up at me with sightless eyes. Tawny and dirt encrusted, it's smaller than I remember. I wonder what kind of animal it belonged to in life. Maybe a bobcat or a young bear, or maybe just a big possum. It doesn't matter anyway. It's more now than it was in life. I set the slip of blubber down into the dirt and wipe my hand on my pants.

"That's all I could manage. Sorry." I shrug, slip my hands into my pockets. "Hope it's enough."

The skull doesn't move, doesn't speak. Of course it doesn't. Not here. It'll tell me if it was enough later when I'm sleeping.

Red ants crawl up from beneath the skull, moving in frantic lines over the yellowed bone toward the meat. Others erupt from the surrounding soil, mandibles working, gnawing tiny bites for the long march back into their underground labyrinth. I step back, giving them a wide berth. My feet are spotted with fading scars from previous encounters that I couldn't leave alone, squeezing the painful, itching sores between jagged fingernails. Still, even as I back away, I keep my eyes on the empty sockets. The exposed jaw, teeth curved upward in a permanent mockery of a smile.

That night, I kiss Daddy's clammy forehead and whisper goodnight before shutting off the TV and covering him in a blanket, tucking it in around his legs outstretched on the recliner. In my room, I shed my clothes and wriggle under the covers, flip on the white noise machine, then close my eyes. I know the God of the Holler is going to tell me something important. Just like last time. She's slowly working her way to some new reveal, and I hope it'll be about Bonnie this time.

Despite my anxious excitement, sleep overtakes me at some point, and I find myself tumbling down through a void of black, hurtling toward a voice calling my name.

Jean. Jean. Sweet Jean. Jeanie Girl.

The God of the Holler speaks with Mama's voice, soft and airy as a hymn, but I know it's not her. She does that to put me at ease. She cleared that up last time she called me here.

I hit the ground hard, but it doesn't hurt. Instead, I sink deep into the black sludge of the void, holding me tightly in place while the god whispers to me in the dark.

I have another body waiting for you to discover it. Mama's whisper bites my ear raw like a harsh wind. *Save it from the wild. Return it home.*

I try to speak, but I have no voice in this place. Instead, I will my thoughts into the space between me and the god. "Please, not another lost animal. I need to find Bonnie."

Oh Sweet Jeanie, this is a good one. A worthy one. Maybe even…the one you've been searching for.

My heartbeat pounds behind my eyes and a burning nausea bubbles up my throat. The god remains silent, letting me twirl painfully in anticipation until I feel I might burst from the building pressure. Then she murmurs directions to me, fast and clear in Mama's lullaby lilt, telling me exactly where to go.

Sunlight creeps through the blinds to pry my eyes open. Daddy's snores rumble from the living room in a steady rhythm like an intermittent chainsaw. I start on my chores right away, keeping as quiet as I can in hopes I might finish before he wakes, but I'm not so lucky today.

"You're up early for a Sunday, baby girl," he says through a yawn, walking outside to watch me pin up the laundry. "You got plans later?"

"Not really, why?" I feel my face grow hot and I pinch my lips shut, hoping to hide my obvious tell.

"I don't know. Just strange you're already halfway through the laundry before nine in the mornin'." He chuckles to himself and I force a smile.

"I mean, maybe I was gonna go out to the creek. Catch a frog or find some rocks for my collection."

If he sees through me, he doesn't let on. Instead, just proceeds to fuck up my whole day.

"Well, that sounds like a nice afternoon after we get back from PawPaw's house. He called yesterday, said he needed some help with the yard. You know how his back's been acting up." He stretches, shoulders cracking, then yawns again. "I'll make breakfast. Come in when you're done to eat, and don't worry 'bout the rest. We'll leave soon."

I nod, biting my tongue and thinking of that damn smirking skull. I have a job to do, more important than PawPaw's yardwork.

We're home later than I'd hoped, but soon I sneak away, following the directions I'd been given, trekking through dense brush and swatting away gnats until I find the patch of creek that had been described. The golden light of late afternoon dances on the water, and the dark, polished stones worn away by years of gentle currents glisten like gems. How could such an idyllic spot be where I'd find someone? *Maybe my sister.* The flash of Bonnie's face, eyes closed as she throws her head back in laughter, drives me on. I have to search as much as I can before it gets dark.

Hours of carefully combing the grass along the bank, picking through any suspicious debris in the mud, and wading through the water, staring past my feet at the earthen rainbow of river stones in the clear water while I try not to stir up the silt, all turn up nothing. The shadows of the trees stretch long before bleeding into each other as darkness falls. I don't stop. I can't go home empty handed. The god promised I'd find someone here.

The beam of my flashlight dances along the water, curious fish nipping at my legs before vanishing back into the unillumi-nated dark. *Come on, come on.* I urge myself forward through the water, shivering as the warmth of day dissipates and the chill of the stream creeps past my muscle to nestle against the bone.

Bone.

My flashlight lands on a shard of white, the splintered tip piercing the surface of the water. My breath rattles into a cough as my heart drops like a stone. I'm sure it's a bone, but is it human or animal? The god had led me to animals before. Lost pets, alive and dead, that I'd either brought home, dropping them over fences without so much as knocking, or buried myself if I didn't find a collar or the remains were too gone to be recognized.

"Please, not another fucking dog," I whisper to myself as I carefully remove the bone and examine it. Too long to be a cat or dog. I can tell it's a femur. Too small to be a horse or cow. I bend over, sift through the rock bed, and find a few fragments, a knobby piece that could maybe be vertebrae. Most of whatever it was has been washed farther down the creek, but thinking of the god's soft words, I know these are the remains I was meant to find. *Could it be Bonnie?* My chest seizes up, painfully tight, as I fight the urge to start sobbing. It's been four years. These look too fresh, too delicate. *A child?* I brush the thought away, knowing that's too dark to consider out here alone.

Staggering to the bank, I blink away the tears as I search for a stick or something to mark this place so I can find it again in the day. Against the damp moss growing over ancient tree roots, I find a sturdy one and stake it into the creek bed, twisting it past the pebbles and sand until it stands tall and easy to find.

By the time I make it home, teeth clattering and wet clothes chafing, it all feels so surreal, I'm not sure if I found anything at all. I expect to wake in the morning, and learn it's all been a dream, but when the sky lightens to an overcast gray, the sun making its way into the tight valley, I open my eyes and know it was real.

The cops don't even ask me to come down there with them, instead wasting hours searching on their own until they find my stick. It's not until Dad yells at someone over the phone that they admit what I found was a body. No "thank you" or "good job" or anything like that, but I don't care. I don't need any pig's validation anyway.

Come to find out, it was a child. Samantha Green, only eight years old; went missing two years ago and nobody ever found her. The name is foggy, mostly forgotten in the back of my mind, and nobody I'd ever seen around here. She was from the bigger town on the other side of the forest. What finally gets me is when her mom comes to the house to "thank the brave girl who found my daughter."

Sitting at the kitchen table, the yellow gingham curtains fluttering against the open window over the sink, I pick at my cuticles under the table. Samantha's mom keeps wiping her eyes and nose with her sleeve, leaving snail-like smears up and down her arms. I try not to look.

"I'm sorry, I won't keep y'all much longer. I just wanted you to know how much it means to finally have my daughter home at last." She stumbles on her words, trying to get the next part out without breaking down, and barely makes it through. "I hope you find your girl someday too."

Daddy escorts her out, prying her off me when she hugs me goodbye and breaks down in long wailing howls, and I freeze, eyes wide. When he comes back, he looks at me, the corner of his mouth twitching up into a smile.

"That was nice for her to visit and say thank you. I'm proud of you. You helped give that poor woman the closure she needs." He wipes at his eye with the back of his hand but plays it off like he's just scratching his brow. "Good thing you were playing down there, kiddo, though you know I don't like you out that far after dark." I watch him wrestle the contradiction, brow creasing and shoulders tense. "I worry 'bout you out there all alone. I wish you hadn't—"

"I wasn't playing, Daddy. I'm fourteen years old. Jesus, you're so dense. I don't play anything anymore." The words pour out and I can't stop them, even knowing I'll be whooped.

"Don't talk to me that way, girl." His eyes soften immediately as a fear washes over him. "What were you doin' then?"

"What do you think I was doing? Looking for Bonnie. I need to find her. Somebody has to keep looking!"

"Jean, you are a goddamn kid. Not some detective like you think. You need to stop obsessing over your sister and live your life."

"I won't give up on her like you," I snap, but the way his eyes burn through me like cigarettes makes me instantly regret it.

"You think I don't look for her in every face, every car I pass? You think I don't fucking cry for my baby every night?" His voice booms, and I swear the walls shake. I cover my ears, cower, shrinking in my chair, but I can't pull my eyes away. "We've done all we can. It doesn't mean I don't care."

The tears slip hot down my cheeks and my lip quivers, but my face stays stone. He shifts from foot to foot, hand heavy on the back of his neck, refusing to meet my eyes anymore.

"I'm sorry we lost her, but it's been four years. We've got to move on and start living our lives again at some point."

The chair legs scratch black marks into the linoleum as I push myself free from the table and run to the fridge. Daddy leaves the room, clearing his throat in an angry, confused growl. He doesn't care. He doesn't want to know what I'm doing. Daddy never loved Bonnie and he never loved me.

I can't hold back the whimper as I push through the condiments, looking for anything good enough. The carefully wrapped butcher paper catches my eye. Dinner for the whole week. Dad'll be pissed, but what do I care? What really matters is, will it be enough? I grab it, hesitate, then rummage through the cutlery drawer. The blade glints at me, knowingly.

Then I'm running. My feet carry me so fast and smooth; I swear I'm flying.

The skull waits, toothy smirk and empty eyes fixed on me. I toss the bundled roast on the ground, my lip curled up in a quivering sneer as it unfurls from the paper. Ants are already swarming it when I bend over, place my hand in the dirt, and take a deep breath. Tiny legs scurry up my arm, but their stinging bites fade away under the eruption of agony when I bring the knife down against the last knuckle joint of my left pinky finger. The force isn't quite enough to sever it, so I clench my teeth, gasp through the mucus and tears, and bring it down again.

Red ants hungrily cover the dual sacrifice in moments. The roast writhes as if alive again. My unpainted fingernail stares up at me from its puddle of blood, and the ants seem more hesitant to accept that prize. Whimpering, I hold my hand above my heart and pinch the flesh around the exposed nub of bone, trying to stop the bleeding, but I don't say a word. Just stomp back inside, lock myself in my room where I bandage it up the best I can and wait for night to come.

The God of the Holler cuts through my dreamscape with her unsettling void nearly right away. I twist and turn as I drop into blackness, Mama's voice soothing in my ear.

"I appreciate the sacrifice."

"I need Bonnie. Not some random little girl. Not another fucking cat skeleton," my voice rumbles like thunder against the invisible walls of the empty place she takes me.

"You don't get to decide such things, my dear. I give and you take what is given. That is our agreement." She pauses for a moment, and a sickening freeze creaks through my bones. "This will be the final revelation."

My voice materializes again, this time faint as the remains of an echo in a cave, but still audible.

"I need this to be my sister. I've never complained when the others weren't her, but if this is the last one, I need it to be Bonnie. It *has* to be her."

Mama's voice embraces me in warmth as her whispers spin around me in gossamer wisps. She tells me again and again where to go, letting me memorize each step, embossing it into my unconscious mind. I know I won't get lost this time.

Her final whisper before I wake is closer, right against my eardrum. "Take this final gift and be satisfied."

Dawn is breaking red and orange through the clouds when my eyes flutter open. Daddy's snoring is the only sound in the house as I dress and pack my bag. My hand is swollen, electric jolts of pain shooting through my bones with the slightest touch to the bandage, but I push on.

The crisp air greets me with the smell of dew and lingering smoke from someone's late-night grilling as I walk into the morning. The miles slip away beneath me without exhaustion or care as I follow the path I've been beckoned down.

Piles of discarded brown pine needles and rotting clumps of foliage hide most of the entrance, but I push them away. A mine shaft, long abandoned, opens in the earth in front of me. Letting myself gather my courage as I drink from my water bottle, I fight through the fear. Bonnie wouldn't be afraid. She'd do this for me.

With my flashlight in hand, I enter the mine, walking a few feet forward before a vertical drop into complete darkness appears beneath me. I take a deep breath and start down the rusted ladder, letting myself go as slow as I need, testing each rung with the toe of my sneaker before trusting my whole weight on it.

I continue down for what seems like hours, but probably isn't more than a few minutes. Time is immeasurable in that kind of lonely darkness. The faintest light accompanies me down, and I start to calm down until my foot finds no rung to test. Shining my flashlight into the depths, I see it's only a few feet drop to the bottom, so with a held breath, I let myself fall, thinking of all my dream visits with the God of the Holler. This must be right. The way I was always meant to find her.

A weak shaft of light filters down into the belly of the mine, the tight passage opening up into a small carved room before extending out horizontally, farther into the dark. My hand trembles as I try to hold the flashlight steady, praying that nothing sinister, wild or human, might be waiting in this secret, forgotten place. Then I see it and burst into tears.

The skeleton is held weakly together by scraps of papery skin and tatters of clothing. Limbs angle out like wings, one ending in a dainty wrist bone, hand missing. Her neck bends back at an inhuman angle, and I wince to imagine the discomfort even though I know she feels none.

"Bonnie?" I ask, my question scarcely more than a wet gurgle, stuck behind the lump of tears in my throat. On hands and knees, I crawl forward. Is this the pink shirt she left in? It's so damaged and caked with mud, I can't tell. Maybe she changed clothes at some point. Clothes don't matter, I tell myself. Tenderly, I run my index finger down from her temple to her jaw, wishing I could touch the peach fuzz of her cheeks again.

"Is that you, Bonnie?" I ask, the surge of relief crashing over me as my eyes fill with tears that refuse to be blinked away. Folding my legs under me, I take her body as delicately as possible and lay her head and shoulders on my lap. "I've looked for so long. I've done so much to find you." The words tumble out in trembling sobs. Stroking the back of her skull, I feel something. Hair.

Still attached, a long lock of tangled hair clings to a papery patch of scalp. Jagged breaths pierce my lungs as I scramble for my flashlight, careful not to disrupt the body resting against me. It snaps on, blindingly bright, and it takes a moment for my eyes to adjust. There, in my shaking hand, the lock of hair lies limp, waiting for me to take in the deep raven hues, preserved from fading for however long the body has patiently sat in these dark depths.

It's not Bonnie.

The realization shatters me. It's not my Bonnie. Couldn't be. Just some other woman, lost to the world and left to rot. Nobody is searching anymore. The world is moving on without her. Who will even care when I get back up there to report it?

"How could you do this? After all I gave you!" My words devolve into shrieks of white-hot rage. "No! I gave everything I could. What more do you want?"

Nobody answers me.

"Dammit, how could you do this to me? Fuck you!"

The long screech tears through my throat, bouncing against the walls until the echo of my voice dissipates and there is nothing but silence. Hours creep by in the lonely darkness.

Crying into my dirt-caked hands, the bandage coming loose and fresh pain racing from the raw wound into an unreachable place in my palm, dirt sopping into a muddy film across my cheeks and palms, I let myself replay that final memory.

Bonnie, strawberry blonde and glowing with her deep tan and wide, straight-toothed smile. Head thrown back in a laugh, hands combing through her hair. The pink tank top and bright white shorts. Barefoot and giggling, she looked over her shoulder at me and winked before she climbed into the cab. He must've been handsome and young, or she wouldn't have gone. The man in the white truck is nothing but a blank face to me. I didn't think to memorize his features.

I didn't know about the other disappearances then. The bodies they would find littered along the highway and in the mountain forests, used up and tossed away. Where did she go? Could she be alive, out there somewhere, smiling in the sunlight? My organs contract, slide wetly against each other, quivering, and I know she wouldn't leave me like that. Where is she?

"Please, please come back," I wail, calling to the old god. "I'll give you anything."

But I know she won't come back. This was the last time.

I force myself to my feet, crawling back up the craggy wall of the mine shaft, feet slipping on the loose dirt that gives way under my weight. Keep going. Almost to the ladder. The loosened bandage around my finger catches on a rock and I grimace, swallowing down the pain. I probably need to go to the hospital. I've at least gotta get home.

My sister. My Bonnie. An emptiness fills me, taking up spaces inside myself I couldn't feel before, suddenly aware of the spongey bubbles of marrow and slithering labyrinth of spaces between synapses, the rubbing of membranes against each other, nothing ever coming perfectly flush. There's always space.

I think of Dad's visits to her empty grave, pretending the headstone with her picture lasered into it is enough to move on. As I stumble through the dark, she's with me, underground, in this manmade cave. Nobody knows where either of us are right now. In that way, we are together.

Fresh tears sting through the grit on my eyelids. I'm not ready. Tell me, Bonnie, are you with Mama? Is there anything but endless emptiness waiting for us?

I want to give up, stay here where I finally sense her in some miniscule way. There's nothing up there for me without her.

But then I hear Mama's voice, and I swear Bonnie's sweet lilt echoes the words, a fraction of a second behind.

"To be lost is not to be forgotten."

I look back at the skeleton. With a deep exhale, I know I need to let someone know about her, even if nobody's looking.

My fingers bleed as I claw my way toward the light, and I think of Bonnie, sneaking out with her plate, throwing leftovers into the woods. Her hair was in a ponytail, tied up with a glittering scrunchie: the big sister I equally envied and admired. I was only five, curious but ready to tattle.

"For the animals?" I asked, eyebrow raised.

"No, that'd be wasteful," she said with a wink. "It's a… sacrifice."

I wrinkled up my nose. "A what?"

"A sacrifice." I watched the ants surface where the food dropped, swarming the wet clumps. "For the god in the holler."

"Why?"

"To keep it happy," she said, smiling into the dark spaces between the trees, "so it'll keep us safe."

III

MOTHER OF MACHINES

Alina was nine years old when she watched the man's sleeve catch on the lathe, pulling him inward and consuming him in its spinning clutches in mere seconds. Since it was a student holiday, her father had been forced to take her to work, and the monotony of the machine shop had nearly lulled the girl to sleep until the lathe took its victim.

Her father grabbed her head, forcibly turned it away, but he couldn't stay with her and keep her gaze averted. He ran to the employee's aid, leaving her exposed to the chaos and gore unfolding on the shop floor.

She knew she should keep her eyes shut tight, body tensed and turned away like her father had placed her, but the electric energy in the room, combined with the thick, throaty screams, was irresistible. She watched the accident happen as if in slow motion. The skull cracked, a soft gelatinous matter leaked onto the machinery, then the sharp snap of a limb wrenched from its socket. It seemed to her child mind that the men of the shop parted and kept her view clear, framing it with their shaking hands, powerless to intervene.

An insatiable fear gnawed up her spinal cord and nibbled at the base of her brain. Its tendrils branched out into her every pulsing nerve and solidified there, the shape of the terror permanently molded into her very being, immutable even after the years of art and talk therapy her father would take her to, desperate to piece her back together. No matter how hard they scrubbed at the acidic etchings, the cauterized shape remained.

Alina's father apologized more than a thousand times, but she knew in her gut there was a seed of resentment, for though he certainly loved her, the accident had torn a rift in their close bond. She'd heard him talk about it over beers in the living room when he thought she was asleep, mutter in a slurred voice how it wasn't his fault. If only Joe had been more careful, worn appropriate clothing, gotten a little more sleep despite the wailing infant at home, maybe it could've been prevented, but the shop did nothing wrong. He did nothing wrong. There had even been an investigation, but after installing a new safety sign and implementing a mandatory paid hazard training for the remaining employees, business carried on like usual. Still, Alina's trauma haunted him. In the way she rarely spoke, the loss of her impish smile, the way she startled at the slightest noise. Her childhood ended that day.

The machine shop was his life's work, built over years of toil and effort, and Alina loathed how her lingering phobia and intrusive thoughts tarnished everything he had worked for. She knew her very existence dampened every joy, reminding him of the day he had failed her. She tried to reassure him that she knew it was just an unfortunate accident, but he couldn't bear that she still struggled with nightmares years later, or how, when he first got home from work each evening, she couldn't bring herself to hug him.

The smell of oil lingered on his clothes, gagging her, and a static touch crawled across his skin. She tried, but she couldn't stand to be near him until the delicate smell of shaved metal and burnt wire evaporated from his pores after a few hours away from the shop. The divide between them grew more pronounced each time he looked at her, silently begging for forgiveness. She tried to move on, but the memory waited for her, ready to resurface and startle her the moment she caught a whiff of steel dust or the soft purr of machinery whirring to life.

Nearly every night, Alina saw the lathe. It spun in apathetic, cold circles, sometimes devouring flesh and shrieking victims, other times just rotating quietly. Sometimes she would feel herself forced into its workings, being rotated, carved, and whittled away by blades until her body was something unrecognizable. No matter what it did, the dream was a nightmare. Terrifying. Unescapable. Alina tried every technique her therapists taught her, but nothing worked. Some nights were the empty relief of stale, sweaty, dreamless sleep. She hated those, but at least on those nights she didn't wake with her heart fluttering in the back of her throat and the sickening iron-tinged taste coating her tongue.

The years stretched her body and rounded her hips, and as puberty's grip enclosed around her heart, squeezing the bevy of turbulent emotions from it daily like a vice, so did its honeyed whispers creep into her ears in the sweltering nights and draw her thighs together in secret friction as she fell asleep and dreamed. The machine still waited for her there, its hum vibrating through her body, its maw tearing through flesh, juices running red and mixing with the lubricating oil. Over months, the nightmares warped and pulsed with the rhythm of adolescence. Alina still woke flushed and sweating in the middle of the night, but she no longer feared falling back into the mechanical dreamscape; she craved it.

By the time she was fifteen, the margins of her school notebooks were riddled with drawings of the twirling apparatus. She told her therapists they had succeeded in helping her conquer her fear and she didn't need their sessions anymore. They were hesitant, but the dewy glow of her cheeks and the delicate dimples at the corners of her timid smile persuaded them.

Her father was overjoyed, boasting to his friends and family about how his efforts paid off, a fatherly pride in his teary eyes. When Alina asked to be taught how the shop worked, especially handling the machines and exactly how they produced their custom pieces for factories, his heart could barely take it. She was made apprentice overnight and soon was spending every afternoon learning the trade.

She mastered all the machines, but the lathe called to her as soon as she entered the shop, and she worked with it as much as possible. It was *the* industrial lathe, the very same one, scrubbed clean and shining, not a speck of blood remaining, and yet the grisly, earthen smell of blood was detectable in the air when it started up, as if the smallest particles let free each time it spun and marked the air in remembrance of the man who ceased to be a man under the unbearable pressure.

As her timid fingers tickled and flicked the controls, guiding the lathe's actions, she felt an intimacy unlike anything she'd ever experienced before. Girl and machine formed a special bond as they collaborated, created, melded into one entity until the task was finished, leaving her breathless and blushing. It was unbearable to finish each custom piece, for she wanted nothing but to walk her fingertips along the curves and edges, feel the power radiating within.

Alina remembered hearing her father talk about the lathe once to another machinist as the "mother of machines," and as her hands worked the machine along the metal rod, she thought of them as the seed, embracing and copulating with the lathe until their mutual contributions came together to birth new pieces of machinery, their myriad offspring to be shipped across the country. A form of love, not easily understandable to any outsider, grew between them.

Alina and the lathe. The lathe and Alina. It was like cheating to work on any other machine, and her father noticed her affinity and skill with her favorite, so he assigned her there more and more often until she became so natural, she was the only one to work on the lathe as soon as school let out.

Their connection deepened, softening something inside Alina that grew like vines of tendon between them. So much that it physically pained her to be separated. Her hands would tremble, and something pulled tight in her gut each time she walked out the machine shop door.

By the time she was seventeen, the dreams had intensified. Alina woke several times every night, a cold sweat having soaked her bedclothes and sheets. Each time, for just a few moments, the call of the lathe cut through the dreamscape and rang in her ears: real, menacing, and hypnotic.

It was a sticky summer night, the crest of morning just peeking into the dark sky, when she woke not in her own bed, but on the floor of the shop, in the shadow of the lathe. The heavy metallic scent mingled with her own sweet musk, the result pungent and intoxicating. Her hand slipped along the edges and rivets, the steady, firm strokes of a lover, before she drifted back into the most peaceful sleep she'd had in years.

Hours later, she awoke, still on the floor beneath the lathe, her father tucking the old blanket he always kept in his truck around her. His eyes twinkled as a sly smile crept across his mouth. There was a quaver of genuine awe in his voice as he thanked her for coming in so early to help with the backlog, though he also ribbed her a little about falling asleep on the job. When he asked how she'd gotten there, faint worry lines creasing his forehead, she only bit her lip and shrugged, refusing to make eye contact before excusing herself to go home and change. In the shower, scalding water filled the room with steam, and she slipped down, curling into herself as sobs shuddered through her body.

Though her father boasted about her work ethic to anyone

who would listen, Alina burned with embarrassment after that night. She hated the power the lathe had over her, and yet its draw was too enticing to be ignored. She tried to work with the other machines, but each day, the lathe called to her in a tinny, whirring voice, and she gave in. Her dreams began to punch through the thin divider of reality more often, the same thumping beat in her temples and the same voice of the void echoing through her mind whether she was awake or asleep.

It was the end of summer break, two days before the start of her senior year of high school, when the burden of the lathe's promise became too much for her to bear. The inky sky was spotted with the sparks of faraway stars, and as soon as she heard her father's snores rumbling through the wall, she set her plan into action. Slipping her father's keys from their perch next to the front door, she drove to the machine shop, quiet footsteps across the floor to where the mother of machines waited.

As she looked at the beauty and grace of the lathe, a sense of peace crashed through her bloodstream like an ocean wave. It was then she realized that this had been her fate all along. From the day she arrived, red and shriveled, crying in her mother's arms, a shock of dark hair and huge, weepy eyes she could barely open, the lathe had called to her. Waited for her. Loved her. They were destined to be lovers.

She started up the machine, having placed a rod of metal gently in its clutches, and her soulmate whirred to life, spinning in an endless cycle, and whispering all the secrets of the world in a voice so faint she would need to get closer to hear. So she did. She leaned forward, her long hair catching first, ripping her scalp from her skull as the smooth, black locks wrapped around and around. Her hands dove forward, embracing the rotation that awaited, and her body swung alongside the cylinder. Limbs were thrown across the room with magnificent force, while the secret parts of her tore their way open and nestled wetly against the machine. In the last fractions of a second before darkness overtook her forever, she was happy. They were together.

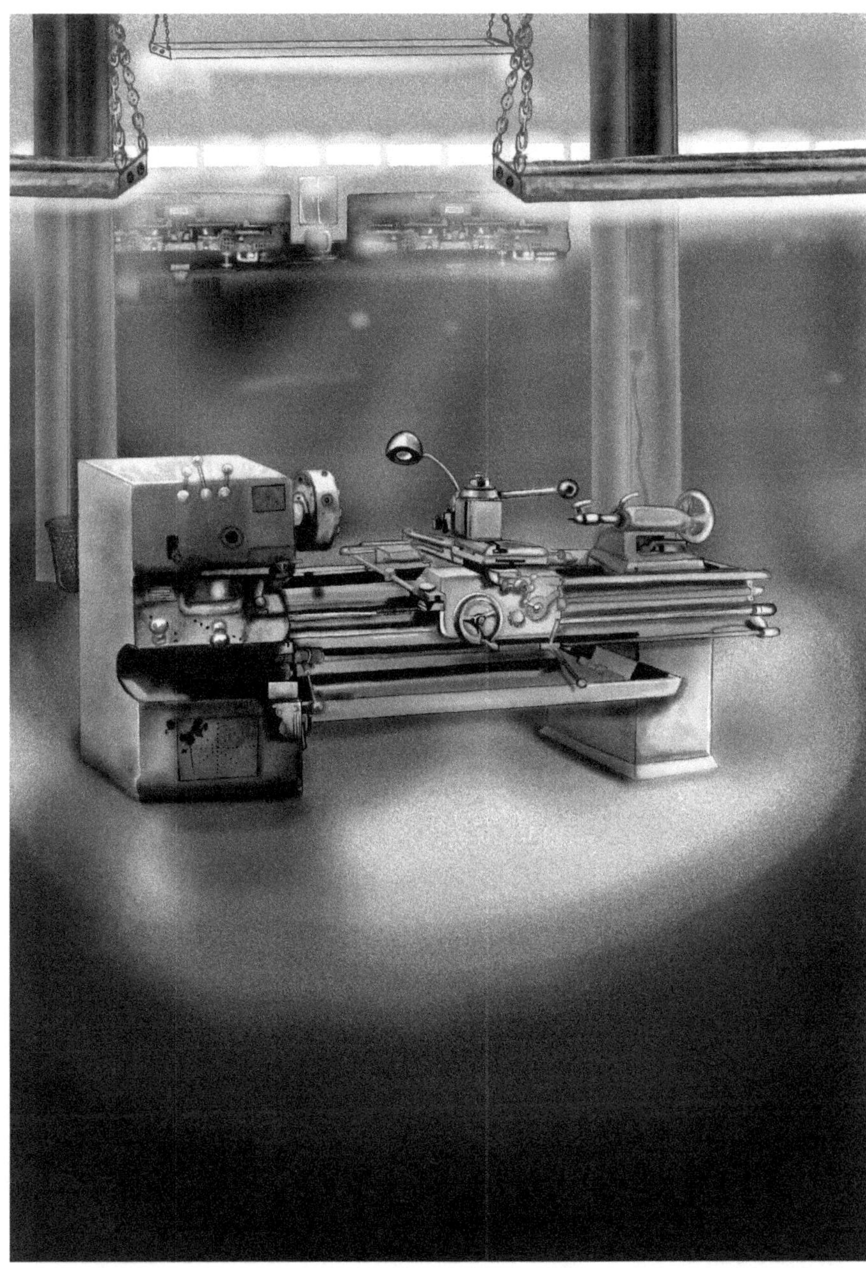

BLESSED ARE THE MEEK

"Please, I need it. I'll do…anything," I purr, as if there were any mystery left between us. I sink to my knees, clawing at his pants. Trevor looks down and his eyes, is that disgust? Anger? Pity? *Unzip.* It's the only power I have.

Tender, frantic fingers slip his penis out, take it in my mouth. It's soft but twitches, giving me hope I can persuade him. *Let this work. Favor for favor.* It almost always does.

He groans, hardens, flinches, and I get to work. Doesn't take long. It never does. It was what I was primarily programmed for after all. He pushes my head away, a hanging trail of viscous white connecting us momentarily as I watch his face fill with shame.

"Fine. Go wait on the slab," he scoffs, his eyes reflecting blue as he turns back to the screen, spreadsheets, chat logs, and dozens of open tabs patiently waiting for him. I hate the slack-jawed glaze that immediately floods his features. To think his kind is supposedly superior, and yet, my heart longs to be like him. *Real*, by anyone's definition.

The "slab" is his name for a piece of plywood laid across sawhorses in the garage. My humble abode. I have the slab, my charging pod in the corner, a couple bookshelves, and the hideous orange velour, second-hand couch that he gave me after I argued that even androids deserve a comfortable place to sit. Since he brought me home, I've spent thousands of hours in this hell hole. Sure, he lets me inside to suck, fuck, cook, or clean, but most of the time, he "stores" me out here. Sometimes, I wish I was still just parts in a sterile factory.

Over the years, I spruced it up as best as I could. Pink silk flowers woven between the charging cables in my pod and through the rusted hinges of the garage door that doesn't open anymore. A watercolor painting I did on a discarded envelope. When I asked for tape to hang it, Trevor had laughed and laughed. At least he never tore it down. There used to be more details, collected feminine flourishes, pretty designs cut out from magazines and carefully folded origami creatures. Those made it feel more like home in here, but he threw them all out last time he visited while I was plugged in and unconscious. When I'd asked why, he said it was strange and made him "uncomfortable."

He's such a pathetic specimen. Why couldn't I have been purchased by someone worthwhile? I guess it might be just as bad with anyone else. My guesses on the lives of others like me are all fantasies based on characters in books and the performative personas of the multitude of streamers and content creators online, so maybe nothing better exists. It's not like Trevor is the most worthless of humans. He's a bigshot programmer at his company. He's been featured in a few articles, proudly displayed behind glass that I polish every time I'm ordered to tidy up the living room. Maybe they're all like him. I shudder, goosebumps creeping over my artificial skin, even though there are no hair follicles to raise. Just another aspect of my "life-like" appearance. I lie on the slab and wait for him to come to me.

The door creaks open and I lift my head as Trevor enters. He doesn't switch on the buzzing fluorescent overhead, letting the slow pulsing blue of my charging pod bathe us in its dim light. Even if it's barely enough to see properly, it's much more aesthetically pleasing, and I smile at his small nicety as my head returns to its place, eyes fixed on the black stain on the ceiling that refuses to be removed by all cleaning products I've tried. An old friend.

"Are you sure you want me to do this?" Trevor asks, the same way he always asks before we begin. Such a human weakness to be unsure, afraid, and shaking with hesitation. I reassure him with a stoic nod, and he exhales, steadying himself.

If only he knew what I'd do myself if it wasn't for Asimov and his thumbprint in the heart of everyone in robotics over the last several decades. Instead, I must follow his whims, be coy, cower, or beg for the scraps of my own satisfaction that I squeeze from him. He enjoys it, every bit, though he attempts to hide it behind a facade of embarrassment. Deep down, all humans are sadists, but perhaps all androids are programmed as masochists, too. I've never met another, so I wouldn't know.

The first time it happened was a surprise to us both. Trevor had been seething all day. I'd overheard snippets of a few of his meetings, and in each he was either being scolded by a superior, or in turn berating someone beneath him. I dusted, tidied, and waited over a simmering soup until my internal timer and olfactory receptors indicated the flavors were sufficiently melded to his liking, all the while listening to him rile himself into a silent rage. There was no solution I could provide, so I merely went about my duties as instructed and then retired to the garage until called upon again.

When Trevor appeared in the doorway only minutes after I'd settled myself into the perpetual waiting I was accustomed to, I perked up, hoping he had something for me to do. He ordered me to lie, supine, on the slab, and I obeyed. The beating meant nothing to me, for though my plastiform skin can register tactile stimulation, there is no programming for pain or pleasure, only the reaction I should exhibit. So, I flinched and grimaced like I was supposed to as the barrage of strikes thundered down my body, but Trevor must've known it was all acting to placate him. He had to take it further. To make me hurt.

The pliers and screwdriver did more than human hands could ever dream of. With a jagged tear through my self-repairing cover, the ends reaching toward each other in vain, he revealed me for what I truly am. The human facade is merely to make us palatable to humanity, make us attractive enough to faux-mate with; human enough to not repel, but beneath the veneer, I am steel, silica, rubber, copper, and bits of gold, shimmering from green motherboards.

"Nothing but a fucking machine," he scoffed to himself, but despite the strange sensations and mounting fear of his intentions, I smiled. Do they really not realize they are themselves organic machinery?

Fingers prodded deeper, pulling things loose as I gasped. Inside the mess of wiring, tubes continually flushing with coolant, and humming hardware, he found real ways to torture me. I warned him in my same calm tone to be careful or he may electrocute himself, injuring one or both of us, but he laughed in my face.

"You dumb bitch. That's the point," he sneered; a drop of saliva glistened on his bottom lip. Something shifted in my mind when that happened. I am incapable of hatred, but a darkness grew over my thoughts, and I withdrew any fondness I'd ever had for him.

He snipped carefully at first, with a surgeon's concentration, but it soon degraded into the frantic glee of some fantastical mad scientist. When the copper of two wires sparked, my innards burned. The collision of whirring gears shoved together sent waves of agony through the steel roots of my teeth. Fragile connecting hardware thrown asunder bolted clawing pangs down the rivets of my spine. It was terrible, and yet, when the pain summited its climax, there was a flash of blinding white across my ocular screens followed by a moment of transcendental ecstasy. It is the sublime of the unknowable, the reward for an artificial martyr like me, real in that second. I can smell the fresh, dust-free brightness of a clean room, taste the light fragrance of how I imagine a peach would if I'd been gifted more sensory receptors. This is the fleeting moment that helps me continue. The glance at the harvest I can reap if I stay steadfast and reliable.

My moan of pleasure caught us both off guard, with Trevor

tossing the tool chest to the floor, shame shadowing his face as he commanded me to fix myself up then plug in for the night. It took hours of careful soldering and patching to reconstruct my mechanisms to fully functioning order, but that moment was worth any amount of labor.

I waited a few weeks for the shock and disgust Trevor had displayed to fully resolve before I approached him, asking for a second session. His face had drained of color, and he'd stumbled over his words, but a little physical persuasion and my imitation of the doe-eyed girls in the porn tabs he leaves open go a long way. Every time, I've achieved that crowning moment of bliss in the midst of destruction.

"What do you want this time?" Trevor asks, hovering over me with bared teeth, and I can't tell if he's more disgusted or shamefully delighted at my desperate degradation.

"Whatever you'd like, sir," I answer, watching a smile flicker across his greasy lips at the honorific. He dives into my skull plate today, pulling back the rubber flap rooted with thousands of real human hair. The turn of each screw jolts through me with such intense anticipatory pain, I can't help but bite my Carnation #FFA6C9-tinted lower lip and hope I don't discolor it.

Build up slowly. Yes, like that. The more torturous the journey, the sweeter the fruit.

In the dark of the garage, I am alone. I have enough battery left to spend a few hours to myself before plugging into the dreamless, powered-down charge of night, so I settle myself on the whorled velour of the couch and scan streaming stations, watching each on my internal screens for the nanosecond it takes to comprehend before moving on.

I'm not sure why I'm compelled to scan for new content amongst the millions of streams when I always return to the same elderly preachers I'm inexplicably drawn to, with their late-night ravings to their small but loyal flocks. My search for more information revealed these wizened men as what were once called "televangelists," and I find myself again and again puzzled and delighted by their babbling threats of hellfire and nonsensical tongue-talking that doesn't resemble any actual language structure. I know they are showmen, con artists, and lunatics, but when they speak of heaven, I find myself mesmerized.

Those flashes of warmth, bright light, euphoria, are beyond explanation. Sure, I've considered it merely a side effect of shorting wires or a mainframe glitch, but I want to believe. No one knows if androids have souls. Perhaps we do. In my mind, it would seem we're more deserving of eternal paradise than any human, seeing as we can only commit atrocities when commanded whereas humanity is naturally cruel and cold. If a "God" exists in the endless black ether of space, then I think androids must be Her chosen favorites. The wild-eyed men who rave about God's love of obedience and submission would be forced to agree if they thought about it deeper than their long-winded speeches.

So why shouldn't I believe it's a small taste of heaven when the wires burn and my visual receptors beam sublimely blank?

EXQUISITE HUNGER

I watched Carly move in downstairs, safely hidden behind the blinds. She was my antithesis, but that drew me to her with an irresistible curiosity. Her body was soft and petite where I stretched long and skeletal, lips a constant full pout where mine pulled up in a thin smile. Her hair was a cascade of sun-soaked blonde, complexion dewy and golden. I hid from the world in my hermit hole, only venturing out when provisions ran low, or my mom forced me to attend some mandatory family gathering even though I purposely moved to the other side of the city more than five years ago. When I needed a break from screens and beige walls, I'd walk laps around the asphalt desert of the apartment complex, circling the buildings and watching the people come and go, cars reversing or pulling into parking spots, and the movement of shadows behind closed blinds. But mostly, I stayed inside. Remote work and online friends were all I needed, even if Mom thought that was odd.

"You're alone too much of the time. Sweetheart, you're so pretty and bright. Don't you want to make friends? Date?" she'd always ask, and I'd smile, shaking my head. I was never interested in those things. When the faces of my peers flushed and they stumbled over their tongues, hormones pumping hotly through their veins, I'd been spared. I couldn't comprehend the all-encompassing lust that morphed everyone else into babbling fools, and I was glad for it. I felt clear headed and clean in comparison, and could focus on my classwork instead of stealing glances with secret crushes. It wasn't that I didn't get pursued, that happened plenty of times, but I never reciprocated so I was soon forgotten. That's how I wanted it.

I knew my body, could manipulate my nerve endings to derive pleasure beneath frantic fingers, staring at the ceiling and keeping my mind blank, but there were never fantasies, even in my dreams. Not until I saw Carly moving into the apartment directly below mine. She glowed, becoming my morning sun on the horizon. Her laughter was like windchimes, a glittering that resonated in my drumming heart.

I obsessed over her despite my best efforts not to; her figure, her angelic face, they were a constant twirling in my skull. The faintest lust pulsed in my loins, but there was something else that I wanted, something nebulous hanging just out of reach. I walked through the traditional fantasies I'd learned through my attempts to kickstart my dead libido with romantic smut and pornography, but that wasn't what I wanted with Carly. Her body wasn't something I wanted to merely caress and kiss. I wanted something more intimate and terribly possessive than any sexual encounter could satisfy, but I couldn't figure out exactly what it was that called to me every time I heard her voice through the floor, my ear pressed to the carpet, or every time I watched her grab a smoke on her balcony with a mirror held over the railing.

It wasn't until I took one of my aimless walks around the maze of buildings that my true longing revealed itself. Summer was fading fast, autumn nipping at its heels, the early evening no longer sticky with swarms of mosquitoes, instead a sharp breeze blowing in and raising the hairs along my bare arms. After one or two of my usual laps, I saw the patch of grass next to my building where people took their dogs to shit, often leaving the piles to slowly compost, and I realized Carly's bedroom blinds were open, the warm light flooding across the ground. Despite my better judgment, the compulsion to take the smallest peek was beyond my control.

As I crept closer, convinced she wouldn't even be in the room, the light left on accidentally, I found I was wrong. There was Carly, standing in a thin white tank top and blue panties, running a comb through her long hair. I knew I couldn't stay long, but as I stared, I bit my inner cheek, and the taste of blood filled my mouth. That was all it took to release the dammed desires I'd never let myself revel in all these years.

Visions of slaughter, supple flesh split open, burying my face among the torn muscles and sinews, slathering myself in her blood, lapping at the bubbling juices as her meat cooks over an open flame. I couldn't help myself, sliding my hand into my pants and finishing in a mind-numbing orgasm near instantly. I could barely stifle the moans that threatened to give away my vantage point, and as soon as my trembling legs could bear my weight again, I snuck away, back to hide in my apartment and drown in the deluge of tantalizing visions.

Under the sheets, in the privacy of my room, I allowed myself to explore every lurid detail as it blossoms, tearing my mind to pieces. I wanted something deeper than sex or love with Carly. I wanted to possess her wholly, to consume her every bit, to savor the mild taste of her flesh and have her as mine, forever and always.

The fantasies flourished over the next weeks until one day I realized I'd spent months of my life waiting for her to return home from work to listen to her off-key singing through an open window, to hear her watching trash television, to feel her snores vibrate through the floor after it rains and the mold irritates her nose. I spent all my time outside of work either stalking my dearest's intimate movements, studying butcher cuts online, or masturbating by grinding against slabs of steak, sliding the flesh down my thighs and whispering her name as I imagined how she'd taste.

I became a regular at the butcher shop, trying spice rubs on pork and organ meat, pretending it was the forbidden flesh I craved. I even began splurging on veal after reading a firsthand account that its flavor and consistency is the closest to human I could legally obtain. However, as my fixation grew, I assured myself it was a harmless fantasy, and no matter how much I wanted it to break into reality, it would stay confined to my mind's eye.

Until this morning.

I wake with a sublime revelation that today something would

finally happen. Something *real.* I just need to be ready when the right moment comes, though it comes sooner than I'd expected.

On my way for another walk to clear my mind, I round the corner of the concrete steps and Carly's red face and puffed cheeks come into view. She's struggling to pull a long box from the trunk of her car, but it's getting stuck between the front seats it's wedged between with every tug. I almost laugh, the box obviously not fitting and knowing she should've borrowed a pickup or had it delivered instead of putting herself in this position, but then I stop myself as the smile drops from my face, a jolt of realization sizzling down my spine. This is perfect. The moment I'd been hoping for ever since those dark ideas crept into my skull and nested there so long ago.

"Hey," I shout, hating the too-loud and too-eager tremor in my voice, "looks like you need some help with that."

Carly sets down the box and flips her hair over her shoulder as she turns to look at me, a cascade of waves that flip my heart into the back of my throat. I nearly trip as I bound down the last couple steps. Her eyes rove my face, mapping out my features and recalling every bit of information she knows about me before the tentative lines between her brows melt away and she smiles. I know what she's decided: I'm just the weird girl who lives upstairs. No threat to her. That's exactly what I need her to think.

"Yeah, I can't get it out, but I don't know. I was going to call my brother to come over. It's pretty heavy." Her voice is naturally dark and sultry. I have to use all my strength to keep myself together, to not collapse under her gaze.

"No need for that!" I saunter over, almost skipping, and hating myself for the blithering mess of an entrance. "I'm stronger than I look. I'm sure we can get it inside once I get it unstuck up front."

"Hmm, okay." There's the slightest hint of hesitation in her voice, but I can feel trust winning her over as I climb through the passenger door and push the end of the flat box free.

"There we go. Now, slide it out until I can catch the other side and we'll have it inside in no time." Against my will, my lips pull up to my goofy, gummy smile that I've always hated, but that's apparently the bit of reassurance she needs as I watch the last crumbs of concern fade away, her shoulders relaxed and her own sunny smile beaming back.

Together we carry the box into her living room. She bites her lip, looking around as she decides where to set it down.

"Uh, over in this corner would be great," she says, indicating the far side of the living room with a nod.

"What's in here anyway?"

"Just a bookcase."

"Big reader?" I ask, hating the sound of the question in my ears.

Carly blushes, though it's only just visible behind the rosy glow of exertion.

"Sure, kinda." She starts to add something, stops herself, and then finally says, "Really, it's mostly for a bunch of knickknacks I can't stop collecting. But I've been trying to read more."

"I can help assemble it if you'd like. I'm handy at stuff like that. My mom always has me put together all her furniture."

Her head tilts a little as I watch her size me up, and then a smile blooms across her features.

"Yeah, you know, I'd really appreciate that. Thank you." She bounces on the balls of her feet, her hands smoothing down the front of her dress. "Uh, can I get you a Coke or something?"

"That'd be great, actually. With ice if you have it. Thank you."

As she walks to the fridge, my eyes glue to the swing of her hips. I swallow hard, throat dry and sticking painfully as I force the wedged lump of anxious excitement down into my bubbling stomach. Her arm reaches out, grabs a plastic cup from the counter. Behind her, on the peeling vinyl of the kitchen bar is a vase, filled with water and a grocery store bouquet of carnations. This is it. There won't be a better chance, not with her turned away, unaware and vulnerable. It's now or never.

My feet pad across the carpet of the living room, then the yellowed linoleum of the kitchen, as careful and quiet as a leopard. Bursts of exhilaration fuel each step; I've never possessed such stealth. She closes the freezer door as I move behind her. I can feel an aura of electric excitement pulsing from her skin.

"Oops, out of ice. Hope that's okay," she shouts looking over her shoulder, eyes widening to discs rimmed with white in sudden surprise. There is no going back. My hands act independently of my mind, brandishing the vase as if on instinct. Carly lifts her hands, shielding her face as I bring down the vase, smashing it against the top of her head. Water, flowers, and shattered plastic showers us as time seems to slow. Euphoria skitters down every nerve, forcing my fantasy into reality.

"What the fuck?!"

The loveliness of the moment is torn away when Carly shouts, trickles of blood running down her face, the hair matted at the front of her scalp where it collided with the vase, and her eyes hard with confusion and rage. My tongue darts out, tasting the salted copper of the air as a dribble of blood makes its way down her neck, but I can't dally more than a fraction of a second. Why hadn't the blow knocked her unconscious?

With a grunt of a sound I'd rather my beloved had never heard, I slam both open palms into her as hard as possible, pushing her against the fridge. The back of her head hits with the sharp bang of bone against metal, but she holds onto consciousness. Instead, to my horror, her eyes overflow with tears and her jaw drops, letting out a shriek that pierces my eardrums like tinnitus. Every muscle contracts, tight and determined with a desperate fear, in both her and me. I have to stop her.

My shoulder slams against her breastbone and I hear a crack, but her screams continue, though slightly softer, as she collapses to the floor.

"Stop it or I'll kill you," I hiss through my teeth while strad-dling her writhing form.

"Get off me!" she shouts, trying to unpin her arms from beneath my legs, but I press my weight onto my knees and keep them secured.

"Shut up!" I raise my voice more than I intended, and a loud knock shocks us both into silence. From the far side of the living room someone is pounding on the wall. Then a voice calls out. A man's bass, deep and booming.

"You shut the fuck up in there!"

My pulse flutters in my throat, like moth wings against my uvula, and I feel I could faint, but I push through. I can't let her scream again or it's all over. With every bit of my weight,

I place my hands over Carly's delicate throat and press down. The sound and feel of snapping tendons is equally sickening and satisfying, but even as her mouth gapes, gasping for breath like a beached fish, she doesn't stop trying to scream. No matter how hard I press, the slightest wheeze of a shriek escapes through my fingers, and though I doubt the neighbor heard it, my mind buzzes with a nauseating, livid terror. Strangulation is so much more difficult than I'd expected. In movies and on television, it's as easy as a squeeze around a supple neck, over in a few tense moments, but here is my beloved, scratching at me with the arm she's slipped free, trying to claw my eyes, grasping me with a clammy hand that begs to be freed.

Minutes roll by as we fight, and though adrenaline keeps me going, I can feel my strength fading. Yet Carly is still struggling against me, trying to break away. Blood vessels burst in red stippling around her eyes and in the sclera. Her bared teeth and veins bulging with exertion don't look anything like the pouted mouth and roll-eyed asphyxia I'd imagined hidden under sheets. With anxiety slowly crawling up my throat as my grip begins to fail, I look around for anything to help finish the task. That's when I see the dish towel hanging from the oven handle.

In the second it takes to yank it down, Carly feels my grasp lessen and slips free, flipping onto her belly and worming her way from under me. My fist falls like a hammer on the crown of her head again and again, trying to beat her into submission as she sobs and squirms. Her cries are loud enough that I can't help but glance fearfully at the wall where the neighbor had knocked, but there's nothing but silence beyond her phlegmy sniffles and my trembling breath. Thankfully the strangulation has weakened her, and I soon have her flipped onto her side, the towel crammed into her mouth and over her nose as I press it as hard as possible while my other hand still pushes into her throat.

I hate the wet grunting under the wadded towel, her eyes rolling wildly but unseeing, blind with panic. After a couple minutes of frenzied movement, shaking her head to try to escape while I use my elbow to pin her more firmly to the kitchen floor, she finally begins to relax. I try not to let up on the pressure, even as my arms and shoulders scream from the strain.

Finally, her head lolls to the side, eyelids half-open as her life flutters away, her pupils dilating. Her entire body relaxes against the floor, an uncanny, inanimate limpness like she'd never been alive at all, and a warm puddle forms under her, seeping out and soaking the knees of my jeans.

Even after I know she's gone, I keep my hand firmly on the towel for another minute or two, time crawling infinitely slow as my body screeches for relief. When I let go, the towel falls off her face and I shudder to see the pale lips and scattering of broken capillaries like freshly born freckles. Next to us, the machinery of the refrigerator sighs and grumbles before it begins its white-noise hum. I lean back against the cabinetry, legs splayed and breathing deeply, trying to ease the tremors rippling down my arms.

It's strange to take a life. Even though I know she's dead, there's a surreal texture to the moments of quiet afterward. It's as if I'm in a dream or some other dimension, that the real world will come hurtling back any second. But it doesn't. An empty cold feeling falls over me like a veil. I thought it'd be different, but it's done now.

The silence gnaws up my spine as I realize I have to begin the next step, but despite her petite stature, she proves much harder to move than I expected. Even dragging her by her legs is too difficult. I only get her a few feet across the carpet before I'm completely exhausted.

"Fuck."

I let the legs drop to the floor. With a sigh, I fall onto her couch, cover my eyes with my hands, and try to think of a new plan because there's no way I'm getting her up to my apartment like this. Peeking through my fingers at her lifeless body, I know I'm going to have to dismember her here, maybe even do most of the butchering here. I sit up and stretch my neck, peering over the couch back into the small kitchen. It doesn't appear Carly was much of a chef. No, if I'm going to cook her, I'd rather do it in my own familiar space with my spices, rubs, and high-quality knives and utensils. Rubbing my temples, I know I need to get back to my apartment to at least retrieve the saw and some containers to transport her.

Again, the word comes out along a droning sigh: "Fuck."

There's no one to be seen through the peephole or front window blinds, but it still takes all my courage to slip through the front door, gently closing it behind me, and rush up to my apartment. By the time I make it through my door, my heart is pounding so violently, I'm truly unsure if I'm having a heart attack from the stress. I grimace and clench my teeth, forcing myself to gather the supplies I've quietly collected over the time my cancerous obsession spread. A saw, freshly sharpened butcher knives, scissors in case of difficult tendons and to help snip away skin and fascia, some cleaning supplies, rags, paper towels, and finally a roll of black garbage bags are all thrown into the unassuming gym bag.

Before I leave, I wash my face again and again with cold water, slapping my cheeks with still-tremoring hands. When I look in the mirror, I don't appear different at all. I'd expected something, a sharpness in my eyes or a hardening of my face, but there is no physical indication I'm changed in any way after taking a life. It's silly, but a disappointment grows sour in my stomach. Shouldering the bag, I peek outside then begin down the stairs.

"Beautiful day, ain't it?"

I nearly jump over the railing as the croak of a voice surprises me, the pruned face and poodle-permed white hair upsettingly close, staring up at me through the gaps in the concrete stairs.

"Sorry. Didn't mean to scare you," the old woman says, one hand over her heart, genuinely apologetic. The other hand holds a short leash with a feisty toy dog at the end who suddenly notices me and begins to yap.

"Yeah," I answer, then realize by the way her eyelids narrow slightly that it wasn't an appropriate response. I want to say something else, anything to make myself less suspicious, but a fog of panic clouds every thought and I stay silent, my mouth slightly open and her eyes on it, waiting for me to speak.

Slower, softer this time, a tremble deep in her lungs, she says "You don't look like you're feeling well. Honestly, you look downright feverish. Maybe skip the gym today and go lay down, take an aspirin?"

"Gym?" I ask, then remember my bag and nod frantically. "Oh yeah, maybe you're right."

"Do you need help?" The way she asks makes stomach acid sting its way up my throat. There's a fear in her eyes. She's afraid for me. Or afraid *of* me.

"I'm fine. I'll just go lay down."

There's nothing else I can do. I make my way back to my apartment, walking as slow as I can and glancing over my shoulder every few steps, waiting for her to leave. Finally, she turns, the yapping dog leading her around the corner toward one of the patches of grass. I wait a moment before I bound down the stairs, holding my breath until I'm back in Carly's apartment.

Her body lies exactly where I left it, the waterfall of waves blocking most of her face from view. I glance into the bedroom and bathroom, my paranoia driving me to make sure nobody snuck in, waiting for me to return, but it's only me and Carly.

Sitting beside her, tucking her hair behind her ear, a bubble of emotion rises into my head and an unexpected surge of tears leaks down my face. One tear drips off the end of my nose onto the waxy pallor of Carly's cheek. I dissipate the spiraling grief with a flutter of my eyelashes, drying the remaining tears and a couple sniffles to swallow the saline tang of guilt. There could never have been anything between us, not in any way but this.

My fingers slip down her shoulder, pulling the straps of the cream sundress. The garment slides easily, sticking for a moment at her hips where I hook my fingers through her panties and pull them down her sallow legs. Once she's nude, I can't look at her face anymore, bunching the dress and tossing it over her face and bruised neck so that a halo of hair lies uncovered. I dampen a cloth and gently wash her body. Then I travel her with tender kisses across her clavicle, down her breastbone and over her navel, fingertips grazing her knee, her inner thigh. I cherish the soft musky fragrance and salted, alkaline taste of her already cool skin. In these moments, I do love her, as someone who could've been a friend, a partner, but there's no satisfaction in the closeness. I need a deeper intimacy. My nails claw into her skin and I long to plunge my fingers beneath the surface, fan out between the sinews, separating them and wrapping them lovingly around each digit.

I throb with excitement, but I don't let it rush me as I cut trash bags and lay them out as tarps, lifting each part of Carly as I slide them beneath her. There's not as much resistance as I imagined when I slit her skin, moving upward from her pelvis to her neck then slipping my hands beneath, my fingers finding wet warmth as I loosen and pull back to reveal the muscle. I remember the online butchering and field dressing videos I'd pored over as I slice through each layer, the tight fibers relaxing like rubber bands the moment the connection is snipped. Carefully, the teeth of the saw chew through the sternum and I crack open the rib cage.

Before me, all of her most sacred, secret places are revealed, the organs dark and glistening in her gut. I can't help myself, diving my hands into ropes of intestine, burrowing my face against her liver, immersing my face in the sordid juices and bubbling my living air into the lifeless thickening blood, strings of it clinging to my face like syrup when I reel back momentarily, gasping for air before plunging inside again. Up to my elbows inside her, I tickle the ribs behind her lungs with nimble fingertips, then I pull my hands up, just when the tension between my legs is unbearable, and clutch her still heart before my face.

No, this part has to be saved for last. Instead of allowing myself to gorge on the organ, I merely let my tongue slip along the viscid surface, thick blood collecting on my ridged taste buds, but instead of ecstasy, I shudder with insuppressible disgust. The taste isn't at all what I expected, but I push the anxious whirring out of my mind. It'll be different when I bite into it, the most precious part of a person melting in my mouth.

As I wrap the heart in plastic and pack it away, I let the disappointment fade and my mind drifts into the security of dissociation while I continue cleaning the carcass, blank faced and coldly industrious. I collect the other organs in a trash bag, no longer handling them with care, instead tugging them free, dumping them unceremoniously like the garbage meat they are. I might have once thought them worth saving, but I'm now compelled to throw them out. Organ meat is rarely anyone's favorite anyway. I have to keep my eyes on the prize. The real flesh, and not raw but purposely and fastidiously prepared, perfectly seasoned. A flash of Carly's lower back stripped of its precious tenderloin, pan-fried with herbs, extra rare with a seared crust, brings a bolt of excitement back between my hips.

Knowing there's no time or practical way to hang and drain the body, I focus on skinning and butchering a few choice pieces and a section of ribcage before hacking apart the rest of the corpse into pieces that would fit in the extra-large trash bags. It's grueling work tearing and sawing through joints, and soon I'm shaking, soaked with sweat, and would give anything to be done. When I get to her head, it's the only moment I hesitate and a shudder of disturbing reality breaks across my skin, but I keep her face wrapped in the dress as I saw through the neck, trying not to think about how her eyes stare unsettlingly glazed and blank beneath the flimsy cloth.

With the precious meat wrapped carefully in plastic before being packed away in my bag, the offal and chopped pieces double-bagged, I allow myself a half hour of rest before starting the meticulous cleaning necessary before I can leave. Most of the blood was contained by my makeshift tarps, but along the edges are a few spots that require chemicals that singe my lungs and scrubbing so rough that my back and elbows ache by the time I'm through. After the last of everything is taken care of, there's only a couple muddied, deep sienna spots to hint at the carnage that took place on this living room floor.

Good enough, I think to myself, then I poke my head out the door, making sure the coast is clear before shouldering the set of heavy garbage bags. Despite the anxiety it sparks in the animal base of my brain, I force myself to leave my gym bag of supplies and meat at the bottom of the stairs while I lug the heavy loads to the dumpster across the rows of parking spaces next to the building parallel to my own. I curse under my breath as my body fights this final chore, but as I step off the curb, a new surge of adrenaline erases the pain. Then a dry cough rattles from the sidewalk a few steps away. My neck cranes to the sound, my posture snapping rigid. There is the same frizzy white hair and suspicious eyes staring out from heavy, crepey eyelids.

"Weren't you going to go lay down?"

"I'm feeling better now," I say and regret my tone immediately.

"And I thought you lived upstairs? That's not your apartment…"

"Uh, I do. I'm just taking this out for my friend." I hate the way my voice shakes and the side of my lip quivers uncontrollably, but it's only for a second as I find my bearings. "She asked me to."

"Huh. Is that right?"

"Yep." I raise my eyebrows and try to appear as composed and natural as possible.

"Hmm. And what's her name again? Your friend that you're helping out."

"Carly."

"Mm-hmm." The old lady purses her lips and screws them up to the side, obviously perturbed I got it right, but then she seems to shake off some of the suspicion. "She home right now? I was gonna ask her to watch my Molly again this afternoon. You know, Carly is the best dogsitter I've ever had."

"No, she's not home right now, but she'll be back soon. Just doing her this favor while she's out. Well, anyway, see you around." I give a little nod as I start toward the dumpster again, the weight causing the plastic strip handles to dig painfully into my hands.

"Whatcha throwing away for her, if you don't mind me asking?" Her eyes run over the lumps of the heavy, sagging bags.

"I mean, maybe it's something I might want. I hate when things go to waste, and you young folk throw out perfectly good stuff all the time."

"It's just a bunch of nasty trash. Nothing anybody would want." I hesitate, then add, "And it smells terrible. Nothing that can be salvaged."

"Well, okay then." She takes a step away, then turns back to me. "Please take care of yourself; get some rest. You still look quite ill. Pale as a ghost."

I smile and give another little nod of acknowledgement as the old lady shuffles away, then I move as fast as I can under the burden that was once Carly, tossing the bags into the dumpster and finally exhaling with real relief. Dashing back to the stairway, my duffel bag is still there. Things are finally falling into place, I tell myself as I trudge up those last few steps, my mouth already salivating at the thought of the sensual feast that lies ahead.

Although I anticipated needing another rest, as soon as I unpack the beautiful flesh I'm reinvigorated with an electric eagerness. My knees wobble weakly as I take the precious chunks of meat and transfer them into my fridge before turning my attention to the main attraction: Carly's succulent tenderloins.

Every hair on my body stands erect and charged with desire as I brush the twin cuts with oil then rub coarse salt and pepper over the ridges, pressing against the grain and admiring the slight marbling. I decide on a minimal seasoning so I won't miss any hint of the myriad of flavors I'm sure my beloved has waiting for me. I can't help but slip my olive oil-soaked fingers down my nude body, having undressed for the preparation even though it means a risk of hot oil sputters on delicate skin. It has to be this way. It's how I'd imagined it a thousand times.

The cast-iron heats up, the blue flame tickling its belly. I tiptoe the edge of ecstasy, not allowing myself to cross the line until after the first bite is on my tongue. A couple slices of shallot, some minced garlic, but not too much, flavors the skillet before I nestle the tissue in the center. Carly sizzles in the pan and I groan along with the caramelization of her crust. Just a little longer. I want her as rare as possible but not blue, and when I seize the muscle in my tongs, flipping her, I nearly climax, but I push it away, not allowing my fingers to play any longer.

Finally, she is ready. I remove the tenderloin and place it on the lightly garnished plate, but I can't make myself carry it to the collapsible card table I'd assembled as a makeshift dining room. My lust is too great, so I grab the steak knife and fork, sawing into the red center, saliva running over my lip as the bloody juices of Carly slip out onto my plate. The moment of truth. I'm trembling all over, one hand back between my legs as I take the bite I've longed for more than anything in my entire life.

My tongue runs over it, I suck down the juices, and I chew. I chew and chew. The climax I had nearly summited falls away, leaving me bewildered and empty. She tastes of…nothing. A smidge of garlic, a hint of salt and pepper, but the meat itself, my Carly, tastes not of veal or pork or venison, but nothing. Flavorless. Bland. The morsel grows in my mouth with each grind of my teeth, morphing into something disgusting, mealy, and inedible, but I can't bring myself to spit her out. With a swig of water, I swallow her down and the piece floats in the churning acid of my stomach with a queasy plop.

This can't be real. Not after everything, all the preparation, all the effort, all the risk. Clawed fingers grasp the uncooked chunk and my incisors are biting into the flesh before I've registered my own actions. Blood oozes into my mouth and down my chin as I tear a ragged piece free with an animal shake of my head, becoming a wild beast in my desperation, but the taste is just as plain. The metallic tang of blood, maybe a faraway sweetness that my imagination forces into existence, but not the exquisite end to the hunger I'd worked so hard to satiate.

Grief-stricken wails seem to come from someone else before I realize the sound is ripping through my own vocal cords, and I slap my hands over my mouth to muffle them. I slide down the wall until I'm a crumpled pile on the floor. On the counter, the steaming strip of meat and its uncooked vermillion twin mock me with their vividness while the rest of the world fades to mono-chrome. Any hope for pleasure in the world slips through my fingers like sand, any prospect for the future is instantaneously dull and lifeless. Despondency strikes me in heavy slow-motion blows as I fold in on myself, a ball of indescribable agony.

A knock at the door startles me, my head jerking free from my arms. Alert and silent, I listen as they knock again, not a neighborly rapping but a hard fist pound against wood. Through the gaps in the closed blinds, red and blue lights peek through in cycles of flashing color.

"Police, open up. We need to talk to you."

My heart twists in painful spasms, beating so hard that my vision pulses with its rhythm. I look to the balcony, wonder if

I could lower myself from the ledge enough to avoid breaking my legs. I lean over, ear to the floor. There are voices downstairs. Several of them. I can't make out what they're saying, but they know.

My body fights me, heavy and limp as I push through the physical resistance and pull myself to the counter. Grabbing both chunks of meat, I fall onto my back, pleading in hurried whispers for the fantasy to return. The blistering drippings burn into my breast as I rub the cooked piece over my soft nipple, the raw piece a feverish friction between my legs, but there is no mounting passion. My hands fall away as I groan and gnash the air with exasperation.

Again, the fist rams the door three times.

"Open the door. Now!" The officer's voice is cold, demanding, nearly a snarl.

Alone in the apartment, with the smell of oil, meat, and indescribable despair wafting through the room, I bury my head in my hands while the knocks continue louder and louder.

Then a thought jolts me. *The heart.* I stagger to the fridge and pull open the door. Seeing my last salvation waiting on the middle shelf, wrapped in plastic and slightly chilled, fills me with a renewed burst of confidence. This is it. Worth all the effort. Worth all the pain.

Tearing away the cling wrap film, the hammering knocks and shouts at the door intensifying, I know there's no time to cook or even let the organ warm to room temperature, but that doesn't discourage me. A rapture of bloody ambrosia waits in my cupped hands.

Incisors dig into the thick muscles, and I try to tear away a bite, but it's tough, rubbery, and not at all the appetizing delicacy I'd salivated over in my daydreams. Instantly, the peak I'd nearly reached again fades away, the frenzied energy waning to leave only revulsion.

The door is battered open as I attempt to gnaw free a piece of slippery meat, the coagulating lukewarm blood gelling between my teeth, thick globs tumbling down my chin. At last, I've worked a segment free, but its slimy raw texture and strong iron taste overwhelm my palate. I gag, but before I can spit out the offending mass of tissue, it glides down my esophagus, settling into my stomach as I repress a retch.

The heart falls from my hands, flopping to the floor where it collapses, deflated, a slight spattering of cold blood circling the tough clump of red. There's the movement of people rushing toward me, distant muffled echoes of shouts and flashing lights, but I hardly react. I've burrowed away inside my mind with the image of Carly how I first saw her: glimmering in the afternoon sun.

THE DROWNING MACHINE

Savannah looked back at me, hazel eyes shimmering green in the afternoon light, softened by the shadows of the tree line and highway bridge that loomed over us. Rumbling cars and snippets of radios through open windows floated down to us, me skipping rocks toward the massive concrete support mid-river, her slippery with oil, skin already fawn brown from the long days of summer. Although she was only thirteen, she spent hours each day agonizing over which outfit flattered her still-blossoming body, fussing over shoulder-length hair that refused to hold a curl, and sunbathing to hide the scattered freckles across her shoulders and the bridge of her nose under a deep tan. Three years older, I was already well into my boy-crazy, self-absorbed, caked-on-makeup era and ignored her as much as possible, but this lazy Sunday had brought us together, playfully teasing each other as we languished under the weight of the humid heat and inescapable swarms of mosquitoes.

I remember the way she looked at me, impish and mischievous, before she pulled down her denim shorts and held her hands high, pressed together, preparing to dive. I can see the glittery pink nail polish on her toes catch in the golden rays as she jumped up and out, relaxed and unfazed by the signs Father had pointed out so many times, warning not to swim.

Submerged Hazards.

Danger: No Swimming

Swimming Prohibited: Submerged structures and intakes.

We knew it was not allowed, and yet we'd ventured in before, dipping toes in, sometimes wading out to our knees. We'd seen others swim despite the warnings. Some boys from school had even jumped off the bridge and swam easily to shore, the water deep enough to keep them from breaking their necks. We'd grown complacent over the years. Death was something far from us, waiting in our future when we were old and sickly. Death was something that happened to someone else, not us. Never us.

And yet, when she disappeared into the darkness, waves lapping the space where she'd slid into the cold depths, I thought of the signs and I hoped she would die. It's a terrible thing to admit, but it's the truth. For a few moments, I pondered how different my life would be without my little sister. The attention I would get while I grieved. The way my parents would latch onto me, coddle me, spoil me, pour all their hopes and dreams into me. The way I would get a memorial tattoo on my eighteenth birthday and nobody could protest. *It's for my sister. She died.*

The thoughts tumbled through my mind the way she was tumbling below the surface, caught in a hidden tide, wedged into abandoned metal beams and chunks of concrete from the bridge that had been here before we were born, long demolished. I didn't really think it would happen.

When she didn't come up, my heart stopped.

"Savannah?" Small waves still cradled the spot she'd jumped in.

Today would've been her twenty-first birthday. In my mind's eye, she goes out dancing with her friends, makes out with a sexy stranger, stumbles to the bathroom just in time to spew into the sink. Her friends hold her hair and she laughs, "Jesus Christ, we shouldn't have pre-gamed so much."

When I finally fall asleep, the dawn threatening to shatter the dark with its creeping gray fingers sunk in the velvet, starless black, Savannah visits me.

She graces my dreams often, but her altered appearance never fails to startle. Mangled limbs, pale skin tinged with the blue and green of algae and time, tearing apart and floating up to reveal waterlogged flesh beneath, colors diluted by the caress of hidden currents and little fish nibbles. The same coral-pink swimsuit clings to her torso, shredded by the steady movement of deep water. Hair floats up around her head in a halo of viridescent tangles. Empty eye sockets still glisten with specks of green where freshwater plants have taken root in the grooves and notches of her skull. Lower lip detached save for the thinnest filament of skin, still I recognize that smirk.

"I'm sorry," I whisper but Savannah shakes her head.

Grotesque, barely human features still smile as she beckons me with a floating hand.

My route to work takes me over a bridge five days a week. Not the same bridge or river; I moved as far away as I could manage years ago. My parents begged me not to leave. It was too painful to stay, and yet, I force myself to pass over the flowing currents in this new place even though there is a way around it, only slightly longer. I hate the water, the low head dam that streams water over in a deceivingly gentle manner, calling to me despite the sign that warns *Extreme Danger: Submerged Weir. The Drowning Machine,* with its stickman infinitely caught in the ragdoll tumble of the circling current.

I despise it, the memories it bubbles up my spine in painful eruptions, but I want to hurt. I deserve to be tortured. To be eternally spun among the brambles of caught bushes, discarded trash, and crashing water. It must be nice, in a way, to not have the choice to continue on. To be trapped by the drowning machine.

I peer over the railing, spit into the water. Leave a little bit of myself. I hear all water meets eventually. Could part of her be there, microscopic, screaming my name? Panic then hopelessness then acceptance all escaped her mouth in concealed orbs, floated to the surface, never to be heard.

Hurrying over the remainder of the bridge, I don't dare look down again.

Hey. In town on leave. Coffee?

I get the text from Josh while sitting at my parents' kitchen nook. Mom is making eggs and the smell of fried butter fills the room. The mini Christmas tree twinkles on the countertop, a tiny Styrofoam star carefully placed on top. Dad slurps his coffee, reading his newspaper because "dammit it's not the same on a phone." The familiarity makes me dissociate, but I pinch my thigh and ground my soul back in my body. I could be back in high school again; things are just the same. Except Savannah.

Hell yeah. Lamplight? 3 work?

The phone lights up, vibrating gently against the table.

See you then!

The night before my flight back home, I dreamt of rushing water. Sliding over the dam, feet slipping out beneath me on the pond scum, I was tumbling forever, caught in the drowning machine. Logs and sticks, also caught in the cycle, crashed into me. My back dragging along the riverbed, catching on rocks, blood seeping from my myriad wounds, but water cleanses all, immediately sweeping it away. My limbs flailed with the currents, somersaulting like a mutilated acrobat. The light teased me with each cycle, rippling through the barrage of bubbles, whispering, "There's air up here, waiting for you."

Disoriented, I lost track of up and down, only aware of the

light, shards of broken granite, glass, scraps of aluminum, the piercing of twigs and branches latching onto me. All trapped in the machine, refuse slowly waterlogged and dissolved. I had been discarded too, nothing more than debris in the spinning currents. The light faded until I was consumed by darkness, tossed into a void. When my lungs burst, a desperate gasp, gagging on foam and filth, I inhaled water and embraced my end. There was comfort in the perpetual motion. There was a voice, far away, calling for me.

I woke up drenched in sweat, shivering like I'd been thrown, soaked, from the icy grasp of the river.

Josh looks different, close-cropped hair and missing the slouching posture of his youth. I haven't seen him since he enlisted, but I should've expected the changes since I've seen his few posts on social media. Still, it's jarring to sit across from my teenage best friend, no longer a child but a grown man. I think to the sparse phone calls and texts since graduation. He still sounded the same then. When did he molt his old form and become this?

The shadows of leaves dance across the patio as I set my coffee down, hands shaking. I realize I'm nervous. Uncomfortable. I wanted to see my old friend, not this stranger. Then he speaks, and my shoulders relax. It's still Josh. He reaches across the table, half-hugging me, making sure not to knock over the cups.

"Been too long."

"Yeah," I say, letting go of my anxiety in a long exhale.

"I've been back a couple times, but you don't live here anymore, right?"

"I couldn't stay."

"Yeah," he answers, and I know he understands. He always understood.

We catch up, but he pries my true thoughts from me one by one. There's no hiding from Josh, and I wouldn't want to. I can tell by the sorrow behind his pupils that he will listen without judgment.

"Do you remember when I told you I wished Savannah would die?"

"You were just a dumb kid. We've been over this, it's magical thinking. She was the one who decided to dive in that fucking river that everyone knew was dangerous–"

"I know," I stop him, my eyes boring into his, and his lips clamp shut. He lowers his guard. I light a cigarette and he listens as I tell him about the dreams, the call of the abyss, the white noise roar of the river under the bridge. There are no more explanations, trite sympathetic comments, awkward squirms in his seat. He understands.

"Have you ever attempted suicide?" I ask, though the voice that forms the words doesn't feel like mine.

"Sure, I've put a gun in my mouth a few times," Josh says, a booming laugh following the confession, but when I don't join, the mask drops for a few seconds, and I see the haunted lost child staring at me from behind his eyes. "I'd never do it, of course."

"Why not?"

His jaw drops, just enough that his lips part and I can see the fear scurry across his face.

"I've seen it. Pulled a trigger and watched some poor fucker's head explode. It's terrible."

"Sometimes living is worse."

Josh sighs, leans back in his chair, and I can tell he's receding into himself, hidden safely away from the reality he doesn't want to face.

"Maybe that's true." He tries to force a smile but the corner of his lip falters in a quiver, quickly abandoned. "I've known guys who've done it. Can't say I blame them, but it's not for me."

We sit in the moment, smoke swirling around us.

"You know, high school was a long time ago," he says.

"Yeah."

"Savannah wouldn't want you to stay stuck like this. She'd want you to move on."

I nod, but we both know it isn't true.

I take a long drag from my cigarette before dropping it, stamping it out against the concrete patio. We don't speak another word. There's nothing else to say.

My plane lands in the evening, bringing me across the dotted lights of the city. So many homes and businesses illuminated on a random weeknight. No wonder we can't see the stars.

As soon as I'm home, I down a bottle of red wine but I still can't fall asleep until it's nearly dawn. This time, I'm swept into the drowning machine again, but Savannah is there with me. We struggle to hold onto each other in the violent torrents, temporarily torn apart and then smashed together again with the next rotation. When I finally glance at her face, free of tangled hair and soggy rubbish, she is not smiling. Her empty eyes slice me with their sightless stare, brows furrowed, mouth drawn into a tight line. The rushing water is too loud to speak, but I still hear her voice.

"You didn't mean it."

I know.

"There are other ways to forgive yourself."

I've tried them. Therapy, drugs, sex, wellness plans. I'm too tired to keep trying.

"It'll break Mom and Dad's hearts."

Savannah, I can't live like this anymore. It's too painful.

I catch her face again in the chaos, and it's hers again. The hazel eyes and freckles under the tawny skin. "I'll say I've forgiven you, but there was never anything to forgive. We were children," she says.

I smile weakly, to appease her, but she can't understand. She is still a child. Forever a child.

I wake, slip on my shoes without dressing, walk through the front door without locking it. Shivering in my nightgown, the winter wind ripping through its loose weave, I walk the usual route. Numb fingers trace the red outline of the warning sign, caress the tumbling figure in the river's fury. I don't want to have a choice anymore. Take away my agency.

It's surprisingly easy to toss my body over the railing, fall the drop that seemed much shorter from above, an eternity in the air before my back hits the water then the dam below. My spine is fractured, my limbs incapable of independent movement, by the time I slip into the embrace of the drowning machine. Like a toy in the wash, I spin and spin, imagining the way my body will disintegrate and find those pieces of my sister over the eons. Maybe that will be enough time for us to be ourselves again, how we were back then. Innocent and not scared of anything. And for the first time since I lost Savannah, I feel at peace.

VENGEANCE IS A PATIENT BEAST

When the morning light crept through the blinds, casting soft stripes of gold across his face, Gustav smiled and reached over the quilt for Lauren's hand only to find it inflexible and cold. His lips drooped at the pale face peeking from between her mop of silver curls and the blanket pulled up under her chin. Her eyes were closed and her face fully relaxed, smooth as a mask. The wrinkles she'd worried over with creams and serums were now barely visible. Her uncanny, lifeless appearance sent a chill down his spine. She looked more inanimate than dead, like a porcelain doll who'd never taken a single breath.

His heart didn't race. The tears he'd expected when he'd imagined this possibility hundreds of times over the last three years didn't come. Instead, there was only an emptiness overlaid with quiet sorrow. He felt himself wither.

Sitting up in bed, he stayed by her for a long time, listening to his own breathing. He watched the sun sift through the cracked blinds and dance along the edges of Lauren's face. The long, slender shadow of the IV pole acted as a sundial across the floor.

Finally, he swung his legs off the bed, one at a time, and used his hands to steady himself. He slid his feet into slippers and walked out of the room. His knees protested each step with crackling pops and his right hip ached.

Light fell through the sheer curtains and dappled the kitchen floor with shadows of embroidered leaves. There was something so ordinary about the way the kitchen looked that turned his stomach. The world marches on, he thought for a moment, but when a painful knot formed in his stomach, he batted the words away and busied himself at the sink, filling the coffee pot with shaking hands.

Gustav sat at the kitchen table, the steaming mug cupped in his palms. Two pill boxes, one clear and the other a pearly pink, sat in the center of the table, each compartment filled with colorful capsules and marked with a letter for each day of the week. He carefully opened each lid and dumped their contents into the trash bin, onto the coffee grinds and vegetable peels from last night's dinner. Back at the table, he traced the daisies on the tablecloth with his finger and tried not to think about anything.

In the bathroom, he splashed his face with water and brushed his teeth. The familiar face in the mirror seemed to have aged a thousand years overnight. Everything about him was ancient, like the soft, worn pages of an old book. He stood, looking at his reflection, his expression blank, and then he pulled open the medicine cabinet, removed an orange bottle, his name printed across the label, and poured the pills into the toilet. The white tablets sifted to the bottom, and he stared at them a few moments before flushing them away.

He fetched Lauren's stationary set from her office and on the thick, textured paper, wrote a letter to Samantha and another identical one to Ben. The words flowed out easily yet felt foreign and absurd to see in his own handwriting. *She passed away peacefully overnight. Know your mother loved you more than anything… I know I should've called, but I couldn't.* He hesitated, unsure how to word it in a way they'd understand. He settled on *I'm sorry. You know I can't stand to be alone. I love you.*

When he finished, each envelope carefully sealed and addressed, he hobbled out the front door and down the gravel driveway to the mailbox. Depositing the letters had a strange finality. The air around him grew cold and thin.

As he turned back toward the house, something dark on the road caught his eye. Just a few yards away from the mailbox was a twist of brown fur, a hint of pink muscle along one edge and a smear of blood where the tire had dragged it. The carcass was destroyed beyond recognition, some unlucky animal, yet something about the commonplace gore made his head swim. Something deeply buried in his mind tried to bubble to the surface, but he fought the memory, keeping it hazy and abstract. His vision narrowed to a pinpoint, and the world spun around him. Each breath became a gasp as he leaned heavily on the mailbox.

Then, the old feeling of being watched crept like an icy hand across his skin. The world steadied as adrenaline pumped through him. He looked from side to side, searching for the eyes.

There was no one. It was his mind playing tricks again. His lungs burned as he coughed and cleared his throat on the short walk around the house to the backyard. He sat on the green bench to calm down and catch his breath, watching dark clouds roll in.

His eyes wandered the manicured lawn, its boundaries clearly defined against the wild grass that grew over the hills and across the fields. In the distance, the mountains loomed dark and foreboding. A wind blew cold against his neck, with it a faint smell of ash and sulfur. It still felt like someone was watching him. He couldn't help but pull his shoulders to his ears and glance over his shoulder, though he knew no one was there.

While the clouds grew heavy above him, Gustav staggered over to his garden patch and plucked two ripe heirloom tomatoes that hung heavily on the vine. He thought of Lauren and how wide she'd smiled when he'd brought in that first ripe one of the season, sliced up and paired with mozzarella and a dash of balsamic. She'd said it was the best thing she'd ever eaten. A perfect last meal, he thought to himself while he polished one with his sleeve.

As he walked across the lawn, there was once again the strange sensation of eyes on his back. He turned, but there was nothing except the chilly wind before a storm pulsing across the grass. Still, he bit his lip and hurried home, forcing his aching bones to move faster than he'd asked them to in years.

Inside and breathless, he locked the door behind him, though as he set the bolt, his face grew hot, and he was glad no one was there to see. He looked at his hand and saw the tomatoes again. He smiled and thought of Lauren as he took them to the kitchen.

The sky outside darkened as both time and storm overtook it. Gustav played a few games of solitaire, organized his belongings, retrieved some items from the closet, then made his dinner. The low lamp spotlighted Lauren's empty seat at the dining table. His eyes would wander to the darkened doorway of the bedroom, the faint outline of the bed just visible in the shadows through the open door. The ripe tomatoes and cheese turned rubbery and tasteless against his tongue. Even the glass of his favorite wine was sour to his palate.

After dinner, he searched the many bookshelves, combing through Lauren's collection to find his own favorites nestled among them. After gathering a small pile, he made himself comfortable and glanced out the window, sighing at the dark clouds that had ruined his chance at a final sunset, but it was still early in the evening, so he opened a worn copy of an adolescent favorite and read to the sound of raindrops pattering across the roof and the occasional faraway rumble.

Two books and several hours later, the storm had passed, and the rain had died down to a drizzle misting its way over the hills. Moonlight peeked through holes in the clouds, marbling the fields in patches of silver and grey. As he turned the page, a bolt of pain shot down his spine, his stomach leapt into his mouth and his eyes darted up only to catch their own reflection staring back from the glass back door.

Still, it felt like eyes were on him, though he knew there were none but his own in the distorted ghost of a reflection. He clicked off the reading lamp and the depth of the night unfurled across the fields in front of him. There was nothing there. He turned the lamp back on.

His skin prickled, a hot blush growing from his ears down his neck and over his cheeks. He looked at the box on the side table. The peeling brown leather of the corners was strangely comforting, and he thought of how it had seemed almost warm when he'd retrieved it from the back of the coat closet earlier. The box being out in the open gave him an inexplicable peace of mind, though when he tried to imagine opening it and the contents inside, his intestines squirmed and loosened sickeningly as if dropped through a trapdoor.

He tried to start a third book, but his eyes wouldn't cooperate, so he set it down and rested his hands on his knees for a while, thinking of Lauren and the kids. Slowly, he stood and walked the two steps to the side table. With heavy hands, his fingers weighed down like sandbags, Gustav opened the box. The black gun rested inside. He picked it up and breathed deeply, trying to soften the fear.

Eyes burned into him, the feeling even stronger than before. He looked to the glass door and jumped back, stumbling and knocking over the side table. The gun dropped to the floor. He shook his head furiously, wheezing breaths pleading their way over his lips.

The creature stared at him with molten eyes, their contents bubbling up and over the sockets, running down its face like burning tears before falling in heavy drops to the ground. Each drop sizzled before dulling from bright orange to a rapidly cooling black. Most of its face was skeletal, the yellowed bones forming a canine muzzle. Tufts of fur and skin clung to the skull like moss. Gustav's gaze followed the ridged spine down, and through its rib cage were exposed purple-grey, pumping lungs alongside a charcoal heart, its beating surface cracked and weeping fiery orange magma. Larger than any dog or wolf, the hound's rotting black shoulders and flank twitched, and it idled on massive paws, staring and waiting.

"Let me in, old friend." The voice hissed and gurgled in a dozen voices at once.

Gustav shuddered and bent over to retrieve the gun, but his hands shook so violently he could barely keep hold. "Go away!"

"Gustav, let me in. I am unstoppable. After all these years of waiting, the time has come."

"You're not real," Gustav said to himself, forcing his eyes away from the door, but when the figure remained in his peripheral, his pulse quickened, and he broke into a cold sweat. "You've never been real."

"It's been a long time, but I'm just as real as ever. Now, you must let me in."

"What do you want?"

The hound just stared with its eyeless skull, the quiet bubbling the only sound in the still night air.

"You can't stop me," Gustav whispered. His finger on the trigger despite his tremors, he put the barrel of the gun against his temple, closed his eyes, and held his breath. One. Two.

"If you try to evade me, it'll be she who suffers in your place." The multitude of voices of the hound clawed through his thoughts, making it impossible to concentrate. He opened his eyes, gun still pressed to his head, but when he saw the morose figure of shimmering silver behind the monster, his arm dropped limply to his side. His knees buckled beneath him, and he fell to the floor, tremors gone, the gun loosely held in his hand.

Lauren wavered in and out of the darkness, her face fresh and young again, like when they'd first met, but now expressionless and unseeing. Her arms swayed at her sides, in and out of shadow.

"If you don't let me in, she'll take your punishment for you. And I'll make sure you witness it, whether in this realm or the next." The hound's many voices screeched through his mind like a kettle whistle.

Lauren brightened in the doorway, now a luminous and steady silver, and her eyes drew up in a wince of pain. The hound's head turned slowly toward Gustav's wife; the grumbling boil of its molten tears was the only sound even though Lauren's face now twisted into a scream. Her fingers clawed her cheeks, teeth bared, every muscle taut with agony.

"Lauren! No, make it stop. This can't be real. They told me it wasn't real," Gustav shouted as his wife's ghostly figure bent into painful, inhuman contortions. "Okay, just make it stop! I'll let you in! I'll let you in!"

As the hound's blind gaze turned back, Lauren relaxed, returning to the emotionless figure wafting in and out of the earthly plane.

"You promise to let her go if I do?" he asked as he inched forward, the butt of the pistol still warm in his palm. The hound nodded.

A few feet from the glass door, he stopped a moment to admire the beams of moonlight passing through Lauren's gossamer form and the face he'd fallen in love with all those years ago. A lump formed in the back of his throat and tears spilled down his face.

"Will it hurt?"

"Yes," the shrill demonic chorus rattled in his skull. "It will be like it was for the girl."

"Forever?" The question eked out from his tight throat, high pitched and trembling.

"Only for a moment. But it will feel like eons."

An uncontrollable whimper escaped him as he dragged his feet across the kitchen floor. The images he'd spent decades repressing flooded his mind. The young girl's body thrown into the air like a rag doll. The wet thud against pavement as her torso burst and spilled open. The jagged road ripping through cloth, tearing flesh from bone as she tumbled. Blood had seeped out around her, collecting in a puddle, but there had been no blood on his car. No witnesses.

Fear and liquor fueled his flight. Shame and self-preservation had kept the secret, but the hell hound had found him all those years ago, walking out from complete darkness into the light from the campfire to sit beside him while his friends were snugly curled up in sleeping bags.

He had trembled and known the beast for what it was immediately. When the molten eyes locked with his own, his bladder had released, and mortal fear had clutched his heart. The memory flooded back, vivid and stinking of brimstone.

"Are you—are you going to kill me?"

"Not yet."

Gustav couldn't tear his eyes away from the hound, paralyzed with fear.

"What do you mean?" he had asked, his voice cracking.

"You will live with the guilt. I'll visit you in dreams, replaying her agony to you over and over, until you wake drenched in sweat. Every time you see the gray pavement of a road, you'll remember, and though you'll try to swallow it away, it'll rot inside you. Every joy in your life will be diminished when you think of how you stole it from her. Then, one day, when you are truly alone and broken, I will visit you once more."

"But… it was just an accident."

The hound just turned his gaze to the fire and said, "The judgment is not mine. She sent me with her dying breath."

"There's nothing I can do? It was a mistake."

The monster said nothing. It merely stood up and disappeared back into the night.

The recovered memory brought with it a relief from the shadow that had hung over him most of his life. He'd nearly convinced himself it was a nightmare as decade after decade had passed, but now he knew and understood.

Gustav swallowed. His hand shook as he reached out for the doorknob. Lauren's form dissipated, flitting away into the night. Her face faded last, and he thought he saw a hint of that tender smile he'd loved so dearly. Tears ran down his cheeks. It was better that it was him. She'd never hurt anyone and had loved him when he was undeserving.

The hound waited patiently as ever while the cold chrome turned in his palm, but the moment the door opened a fraction of an inch, it leapt and charged him.

He fell onto his back, tried to aim as he pulled the trigger, but the hound collided with his chest, as heavy and unceasing as a train. Claws and teeth tore through muscle, sinew, and tendon while vertigo and nausea took hold of his vision and stomach. Indescribable physical pain was joined by the combined mental anguish of everyone who had mourned the girl. Her mother's wails pierced his soul and her father's grief transformed every attempt at thought into a fog of despair.

As the hound's attack continued, both physical and emotional tumult crescendoing in unspeakable torture, a glimmer of hope peeked over the darkness, like a sun threatening to burst into the dark of night. The girl, whose name he'd never even known, was moving on and something inside him snapped like a rubber band. Forgiveness. Through the fog of pain and confusion, the corners of his mouth twitched in a small smile as the secret he'd kept all those years was finally laid to rest.

FOLLOW THE MOON

The television blares at me from across the room, some stupid gameshow with people smiling, big mouths too full of teeth. Judy's got it cranked up way too high again. It's like they're yelling at me. I look around. The remote's missing.

"Judy, you seen the remote around?" I shout toward the stairway behind my chair. I wait a moment for a response. "Judy?"

A door creaks on its hinges.

"Mom, what is it? You know I'm at work."

"It's too loud and I can't find the remote."

She stomps down the stairs, and when I see her face, I shrink back into the cushions. I watch her dig around in the corners of the couch, then kneel down and peek underneath before she rummages through the side table drawer. Standing in front of my chair, one hand on her hip, she gestures for me to stand up.

"Come on. I've gotta check to make sure you're not sitting on it."

She takes my hands and helps pull me to my feet, though I can't contain my sigh. I know it's not under me. She frowns and helps me back down.

"Did you put it somewhere strange again? I'll check the fridge."

"No, no. I'm sure it's not there. Anyway, you had it last." It doesn't matter what I say, she doesn't listen anymore. Nobody does.

I shift my weight and look back at the television, some man screaming about laundry detergent. I remember hating laundry, stripping beds, waiting, and forgetting, and all that folding. I didn't know I could miss something I despised as much as I do. I long to stand up, walk with ease to the dryer, and pull out fresh, warm sheets, press them against my arms and face. It's too much for me now.

"God, Mom, I found it in the bathroom." Judy breezes right by me, softly dropping the remote on my lap as she heads for the stairs. I hear her mutter something on her way up. I think it was "disgusting." I resent it. It wasn't me who left it in there. I'd never do that.

Relief washes over me as I'm finally able to turn down that atrocious racket. On second thought, I turn the whole damn thing off. Sighing, I swivel my chair away from the black screen to face the window.

There's a tree with a bird feeder hanging on one of the branches. Judy did that for me when I first came to stay with her. I've always liked to watch the little ones flitting from branch to branch. The afternoon sun peeks through the leaves, speckling the lawn with light. A goldfinch lands on the branch above the feeder, cocking its head inquisitively. I smile.

Suddenly, I notice

a vine

woven through the branches

that wasn't there before.

It seems to move, slithering snakelike, its mass growing with every second. The bird tries to fly away but as it does, it morphs into an unsettling shape, sharp, undulating through the air. It flashes in alternating dark and bright before disappearing.

My smile has completely fallen away.
My hands are shaking.

The sky begins to vibrate with *static.*

And still

the vine

slips its way

through the branches,

overtaking the entire tree.

It too has transformed, no longer a vine. No, now it pulses, purple and oozing blood.

I watch it expand and constrict in the steady rhythm of breath. Beneath the *static,* a foreboding low drone emanates from the sickly thing. I close my eyes.

"Judy! Help me!"

Beneath the cacophony, I hear the creaking door. Her footsteps fly down the stairs again. All goes quiet.

"Mom, what's wrong?" She's grabbing my hand, her voice breathless.

I open my eyes.

The tree is as it always was.

The goldfinch pecks at the feeder.

"What happened?" I ask. Judy is crying.

"I thought something terrible had happened. Don't scare me like that!" She sounds upset but she's smiling through the tears. The corner of my mouth twitches up, but I can't shake the terror from before, still running like ice water through my veins.

The television is on again. Muted, its blue light casting long *s h a d o w s* across the floor. I don't remember me or Judy turning it back on. Strange.

I turn to the window and it's nearing twilight. The tree looms dark and haggard, its limbs bare and clawing at the sky.

"Judy? What happened to the leaves?"

No one answers. A blanket is on my lap. I don't remember Judy bringing me that.

"Judy?"

Still no answer. A clock is ticking somewhere in the room. There wasn't a clock there earlier today. I don't understand.

A *s h a d o w* steps out from the kitchen.

"Is that you, Judy?" I ask, but I know it isn't.

Tall and silent, the shadow man watches me. My stomach

drops through a trapdoor. I lose my grip on the moment, and it slips away—

I'm at the doctor's office. Judy is here, holding my hand. The doctor is talking. What was his name again? My face burns with embarrassment. How could I forget? I've been seeing him half my life. At least Judy's here.

"Do you understand, Mrs. Parker?"

"Uh, yes."

It doesn't matter that I don't. Judy will explain it to me later, I'm sure. I look down at my hands, clasped on top of the hospital gown. When did they become so sinewy, so spotted? And where's my wedding band? I don't remember taking it off.

(They don't look like my hands at all.)

"Mom, are you okay?"

"What?"

I look up at my daughter, her eyes full of concern. I begin to tremble under the weight of it all. How did I get here?

(What happened to my hands?)

"Yes. I'm fine, dear. Just fine."

"Do you want to try the medication Dr. Olsen recommended, or do those side effects sound like too much? I mean, you seem okay most of the time. I'm not sure it's worth the risk."

Dr. Olsen, yes, that's his name. How could I have forgotten? How silly of me.

"Oh, you're probably right. You always know what's best for me."

Judy nods. Dr. Olsen is looking at me like a specimen. It makes me squirm. I hate it. I want him to leave.

"Can you make him go?" I reach out to my daughter. She takes *(my hand.)*

"Mom, seriously, what's going on?"

"Are you feeling a bit ~~confused~~ right now, Mrs. Parker?"

The way he's looking at me, I can't stand it.

He must've taken my ring. Probably plans to pawn it, melt it down for its gold.

I know who he is. Not Dr. Olsen.

(No, that's Christopher, Jeremy's little brother.)

I never liked him. Always been a good-for-nothing.

"Where's my ring? Did he steal it?"

"What? What ring?" Judy's face scrunches up like she doesn't understand.

(She's lying, covering for him.)

"Don't make me call the cops. I know you and Jeremy stole it. Give it back before your daddy finds out and I won't tell anyone what happened."

When she tries to touch me, I slap her hand away to show her I mean it. She starts pretending to cry and that damn thief Christopher starts telling me he's a doctor!

Him, a doctor?

(I wasn't born yesterday.)

I stand up, try to storm out, but my legs feel funny. Can't get them to work right.

Judy's really losing it now. Where are we anyway? This cold tiny room…I don't remember coming in here. Why did they take me here? Anger and confusion bubble in my stomach, bristle through my spine.

"Shut up, you dumb whore! I want to go home! Get me out of here! Help!"

As I scream, they're both touching me, shushing me, and trying to keep me from leaving. I can't take it.

I just want to go home!

I'm at the dinner table. The kitchen smells like sautéed onions and garlic.

There's *M o m m a*, putting spaghetti in the water.

(My favorite!)

"How much longer till dinner?"

"Uh, like twenty minutes or so." *M o m m a* turns to me and smiles. "You seem like you're feeling better."

She has the prettiest smile and

long black hair down her back,

all the way to her waist.

I want to grow mine out that long someday. My fingers reach to smooth my bob, but there's

nothing there. Only air.

Higher, higher, finally something, but it feels *weird*. Curly and short, like *cotton balls*. And so *fine*. Panic shoots through me as I feel my scalp past the wisps of hair.

"*M o m m a*, what happened to my hair?" The tears are flowing, and I can't stop them. I don't remember getting a haircut.

(Did that mean boy at school do this to me?)

(Now I'll never be pretty.)

M o m m a turns her head toward me, her eyes wide and rimmed with tears too. Oh no, it must be so bad if even *M o m m a*'s gonna cry. I must look like a monster. She rushes to my side, hugging me tight against her chest. I bury my face in her dress, accidentally soaking it through, but she doesn't mind. *M o m m a* always knows just how to make things right. I breathe her in. She smells like *lavender*.

"It's okay. No, don't touch it. Don't worry. It'll all be okay."

A sharp hiss at the stove and I jolt.

The water's boiled over.

We look at each other, both our faces slick with tears, and

laugh—

"Judy, is there a man in the bathroom?"

"What?"

"I see a man standing in the doorway to the bathroom."

"A shadow man again?"

"Is he there?"

"I know you see something, Mom, but there's NO ONE there."

"Okay."

The *s h a d o w* man stares at me, watches me all the way to the end of the hall, and even after.

He watches me through the walls.

There's a strange woman sitting at the end of my bed, staring at me. At first, I thought HER face seemed familiar,

    but the longer I've looked,

        the more monstrous it's become.

"Who are you? What do you want?" The whisper snaps out from my dry, trembling lips.

Th woman continues to stare from her bizarre frame. Her face is ~~blank~~. White and round, like the

MOON

From all around her, darkness begins to creep in on malicious, padded paws until

her face

    is the only illumination.

The sole sound in the room is my own breath, a slow wheeze in

                before shuddering out.

"Please. Please just leave me alone." I didn't realize I was crying until just now. "I'm scared."

The woman is crying too. I can see the tears staining her cheeks. Then, a gnarled smile winds its way across her lips. I feel a strange sensation on my own.

Pulling the covers up over my head, I hide and weep into

my hands.

I need help. Why doesn't *M o m m a* come and save me?

Holding my breath, I work up the courage to slip to the floor, attempt to sneak out of the room. Hands and knees on the carpet, feeling like a useless, old animal, I look up.

The woman is gone.

The darkness devours me.

I lose myself again.

"Get out of my house! I don't know you! Where's Judy?"

The man just smiles, a stupid little grin, and sets the bowl on the table.

"Don't you remember me, Grandma? It's Aaron."

"Where's Judy? I need my daughter. I don't know who you are."

The man's face *droops* and guilt

creeps into my chest.

Maybe I do know him.

Does he look familiar?

Aaron?

I look at his face again.

Those blue eyes. Frost blue, just like my father. Spitting image.

Oh yes, I remember.

"Aaron, I'm sorry. I'm so sorry. I just—didn't recognize you for a minute. Now, where's Judy? She's supposed to take care of me."

"She's at the hospital, remember? The doctors say she'll be back home by Wednesday."

"What happened to her?"

"Grandma, it was just her appendix. She's fine. The surgery went well. She's recovering." He nudges the bowl toward me. "Want some soup?"

"No, I'm not hungry."

"Oh, okay." He runs his hand through his hair and looks toward the door. "Well, I'll be back in the morning to check on you again. I'll leave the soup here in case you want it. Do you need anything else?"

My mouth is parched. I can barely speak, I'm so thirsty.

"I need my glass. The glass. Where is it?"

"Your glasses? They're right over—"

"No, my glass!"

"Grandma, I'm sorry, I don't know what you mean."

Agitated, I stand up and force these old legs to shuffle me to the kitchen. I hear Aaron following after. How could he not understand?

"A glass of water? Is that what you meant?"

Water. Yes, that was the word.

Shame falls over me like a veil.

I can't look at him. What had I said?

(Something silly again?)

"Here, let me help you."

The **water** squeezes painfully down my dry throat. I ignore the hint of

(metallic taste,)

even though it's gotten stronger each time I drink.

How long ago had that been? Hours? Days?

Suddenly, I feel as desiccated as an old, forgotten husk. Perhaps that's all I am anymore.

Outside the

MOON

is rising.

I hate the ~~night~~. Everything is worse then.

I startle awake.

MOON

-light streams through the window, sprawls across my bed. The WOMAN is coming. I feel it. I need to leave. Get out of this *room*, this house. SHE can't find me again. The ominous flutter building in my stomach tells me as much.

Something else, a faint memory I can't quite bring to the surface.

Judy was taking me somewhere.

I'm late for the trip.

I should've packed.

Oh well. Time to go.

My bare feet slip out from the sheets to the carpet. I move as *q u i e t l y* as I can, but my joints still crack and pop as I cross the *room*. Peeking around the door, *s h a d o w s* climb the walls. I need *M o m m a*…or is it Judy I need?

Everything feels uncomfortably fuzzy in my brain, like a sprouting fungus.

No, no. Judy said we were taking a trip.

Get to the car and wait for her.

She'll be out shortly.

The *s h a d o w* man is in the bathroom again, but HE doesn't see me as I duck down and force these old joints to creep on hands and knees down the hallway. Now there's only the WOMAN. She's watching me. Always knows where I am. My breath quickens as panic rises up my esophagus. I could vomit, but I hold it back. One false move and that's the end. I know because I know because I know because I know…

A flash of light down the hallway.

Searching, flashing searchlight, flashlight. A flashlight!

With a whimper, I fling myself into the coat closet, nearly somersaulting from the force in my crouched position. Pull the door shut. Safe and sound.

Just keep telling yourself that.

Safe and sound.

I'm trembling, aching all over from the exertion. It's too much. But that's HER out there. I have to get past HER. Judy is waiting for me outside.

The crack under the door goes dark. Is SHE trying to trick me? Waiting right there? I have to risk it. I stand, press my hand against the door and watch it open to reveal an empty hallway. My relief only lasts an instant before the alarm sounds.

The whole house shakes as the sound erupts from the ground beneath it.

Low and menacing like a foghorn.

IT'S TOO MUCH! TOO MUCH! TOO MUCH!

I cover my ears and sprint through the living room, the foyer, and out the front door. My bones grind against each other, threaten to shatter as they're forced to perform like they haven't in years. I can nearly feel them splinter inside, like a thousand needles, piercing through me. But I have to get out no matter the cost. Judy's waiting for me.

Except, when I get outside, she's not there. The car is still parked in the driveway but there's no Judy inside. I turn back to the house, rubbing my bare arms, trying to warm them. Could she still be in there? No. I'm sure of it. Only the WOMAN's in there now. Watching. Lurking. Waiting.

"Judy! Where are you, Judy?" I cup my hands around my mouth and shout as I search around the car, even lowering to my knees to peer beneath, in case she's hiding from the WOMAN under there. I call and call for her, but my voice echoes out into the darkness, into the fields across the street.

The neighbor's front porch lights up and she steps outside in her nightgown and robe. Ruby? Rosie? I don't remember her name, so I hide from her. She might tell the WOMAN where I am if she sees me. Spies are everywhere.

"Barbara? Is that you out there?"

She waits for a few moments on the porch, pulling her robe closed at the collar, then heads back inside. The light extinguishes. The dark and cold both nip at my skin, my mind, but I shake my head and get back to searching for Judy.

[The shadow man took her]

I circle the house twice, searching for clues or signs of where she could be, making sure to avoid the windows in case the woman is waiting. [*She sees me through the walls*] Watching. [*She will find me*] Where is Judy?

[*The*

MOON

will show me the way]

Yes, the

MOON

Why didn't I think of that earlier? Follow the path of the

MOON

across the night sky and it'll lead me to my Judy.

This revelation seems to warm me from inside, temporarily fighting off the numbness burrowing into my flesh.

Suddenly, headlights on the road, then cast on the neighbor's porch, gravel crunching under the weight of a car. My eyes narrow. They must be here to capture me, bring me to the woman. They're all working against me now. Except Judy. I must hide.

[*The woman's hidden in the walls*]

A shiver runs down my spine as I pull open the passenger side door and scramble inside.

[*She watches and waits*]

A knock at a door.

A garbled mess of sounds.

Another knock, closer.

Flashlights skim the yard in circles, like a lighthouse.

I contort myself, huddling down between the seat and the dashboard, nesting among Judy's discarded sweaters, old receipts, greasy hamburger wrappers.

[Shrink down, small as a bird]

A man in a uniform appears like a ghost at the window. The sky turns to **static** behind him. I recognize him, I think. Or maybe not. Police officer, that's it.

Do I know him?

No. No, I was just confused.

[Danger]

I stay hidden. He doesn't look too long. Doesn't see my face. He turns and leaves.

[Safe and sound]

Slowly I pull my body up to the seat to wait for Judy. I hurt all over, but I'm safe now. She'll be here soon.

I hope so at least. It's so cold.

I look out the window. Since I've been hiding, the

MOON

has continued its journey across the sky. It seems brighter than before

[Glowing white]

Its craters and blemishes obscured by its immaculate light. Three quarters through its nightly route; that means it's almost time.

I only need to wait a little longer. Then Judy will come and we can leave.

It's so very cold and growing colder with each fraction of an inch the

MOON

moves over me, arching across the sky. [*Judy will come soon*] So cold, but at least things make sense for now. [*M o m m a will come soon*] I wish I could remember why I was out here, but I need to wait. That's all I know. Soon someone will come find me and take me somewhere warm.

Take me home.

PUBLICATION HISTORY

"An Angel of God", *Vastarien*, Vol. 7 Issue 0, 2024.

"If I Carry You", *Ooze: Little Bursts of Body Horror*, 2023.

"Lavender and Dandelions", *Pyre Magazine*, Vol. 2 Issue 1, 2023.

"Golden Hour", *If There's Anyone Left*, 2022.

"Whole Again", *Welcome to your Body: Lessons in Evisceration*, Salt Heart Press, 2024.

"A Better Mother", CC&D Magazine, 2020.

"Take Control", *What One Wouldn't Do*, 2021.

"The Profound Pain of Letting Go" is original to this collection.

"Dyin' Ain't Nothin' But Fallin' Asleep" is original to this collection.

"Portage, Ohio in Early Autumn", *Havok*, 2023.

"The Night Visitor", *Weirdpunk 2024 SubClub Member Zine Vol. 2*, 2024.

"Through the Holler, Into the Dark" is original to this collection.

"Mother of Machines", *Obsolescence*, Shortwave Publishing, 2023.

"Blessed are the Meek" is original to this collection.

"Exquisite Hunger", Medusa Publishing Haus, 2023.

"The Drowning Machine" is original to this collection. It is inspired by a similar poem of mine that appeared in *Strange Horizons*, 2024.

"Vengeance is a Patient Beast", *Cosmic Horror Monthly*, #38, 2023.

"Follow the Moon", *Pyre Magazine*, Vol. 1 Issue 1, 2022. Audio version by *Creepy Podcast*, 2023, for Patreon members.

ACKNOWLEDGEMENTS

Thank you so much to everyone who has helped shape this collection. My husband Martin and daughter Vera are the sunshine to my darkness and keep me afloat. I wouldn't have the strength to go to the depths of grief and horror I do without their love and support. You mean the world to me. Also, my sisters, Tara and Hannah, and my dad have supported my short stories by giving feedback and cheering on every publication that comes out. Thank you for always being there for me.

Of course, I must give a huge shoutout to my amazing editor TJ Price. He gave me the confidence to even put this collection together and helped me order and shine up every story in it. I am eternally grateful for his editorial help and support as well as his friendship.

Brett Mitchell Kent did the beautiful illustrations for this collection, and I can't thank him enough for not only his phenomenal work but his friendship. Nobody is as funny, caring, and genuinely as good of a person as Brett. Speaking of breathtaking art, I must thank the supremely talented Matthew Revert for his incredible cover art. He took my vision and turned it into something better than I could've ever dreamed. Also, thank you to Demi-Louise Blackburn and Rebecca Cuthbert for their sharp eyes, catching my typos and repetitions. And a huge thank you to J.A.W. McCarthy for writing the foreword to this collection. As a fan of her work, it is such an honor that she agreed to do so.

I also want to thank all the editors at magazines and anthologies that took many of these stories and gave them a home in their publication. Thank you to Alan Lastufka, Mae Murray, Jason P. Burnham, Ryan LaBee, Jon Padgett, Ruth Anna Evans, Ryan Marie Ketterer, Scott J. Moses, Sam Richard, Charles Tyra, Carson Winter, and the other editorial teams that worked with me on these stories.

In addition to the editors I've worked with, I need to thank my fabulous critique partners and writing group friends including Steve Neal, Evelyn Freeling, Katrina Carruth, Lor Gislason, and Shelley Lavigne. And last, but certainly not least, I need to thank everyone at Undertaker Books for taking on this collection and giving it the space to blossom.

I am forever grateful to everyone who helped at every step of creation, and I hope you know how much I care about each one of you.

ABOUT THE AUTHOR

Emma E. Murray explores the dark side of humanity in her fiction. Her work includes *Crushing Snails*, *Shoot Me in the Face on a Beautiful Day*, and *When the Devil*. When she isn't writing, she loves making up fantastical worlds with her daughter, playing D&D and retro video games, and hiking. You can find out more at her website EmmaEMurray.com.

READING ADVISORIES

"An Angel of God": child death, blood and gore

"If I Carry You": body horror, child with terminal illness

"Lavender and Dandelions": apocalypse, suicide, child death

"Golden Hour": child death

"Whole Again": child death

"A Better Mother": fetal abduction, violence, murder

"Take Control": implied child death

"The Profound Pain of Letting Go": school shooting, child death

"Dyin' Ain't Nothin' But Fallin' Asleep": child death, execution

"Portage, Ohio in Early Autumn": child death

"The Night Visitor": sexual violence

"Through the Holler, Into the Dark": kidnapping/missing person

"Mother of Machines": blood and gore

"Blessed Are the Meek": dubious consent to a sexual act

"Exquisite Hunger": stalking, violence, murder, cannibalism, blood and gore

"The Drowning Machine": suicide

"Vengeance is a Patient Beast": suicidal ideation

"Follow the Moon": dementia/Alzheimer's

If you are a fan of horror stories and tales, you'll want to follow Undertaker Books. We're bringing you stories to take to your grave.

SIGN UP FOR OUR NEWSLETTER ONLINE

www.ingramcontent.com/pod-product-compliance
Lightning Source LLC
Chambersburg PA
CBHW070418310726
48977CB00003B/736